Dare to Breathe

By: Tina Maurine

This book is a work of fiction. Names, characters, places and incidents are products of the author's imagination and are not to be construed as real. Any resemblance to actual events, locales, organizations, or persons living or dead, is entirely coincidental.

COPYRIGHT

Ordering Information:

Quantity sales. Special discounts are available on quantity purchases by corporations, associations, and others. For details, contact the publisher at the address above.

Orders by U.S. trade bookstores and wholesalers. Please contact Trient Press: Tel: (775) 996-3844; or visit www.trientpress.com.

Printed in the United States of America
Publisher's Cataloging-in-Publication
data Maurine, Tina
A title of a book :Dare to Breathe
ISBN Hard Cover:978-1-953975-16-4
        Paperback: 978-1-953975-17-1
        E-book: 978-1-953975-18-8

Dedication

To my family:
Thanks for your continued support and love.
I love you bigger than the universe!

To Bec:
You're eyes were the first ones who read this, believed it
was worth sharing, and encouraged me to move forward.
Love Ya Lady!

Thank you is not enough.
XOXO

Prologue

I carefully shifted my weight from one butt cheek to the other, shifting my hips ever so slightly so as not to make a single noise, trying to get the blood flow back into my legs. The men on the other side of the wall must have left the classroom seeing as how now the 'others' had gone quiet. If I strained my ears with all my might I could catch a couple of voices whispering in panicked and scared rushes. I listened for just a minute before the shear effort of trying to decipher the cryptic syllables I heard took their toll on me and the threat of a headache precariously teetered.

I rolled my neck in gentle circles trying ever so silently to get a good stretch in while I still had the chance. I bent the slightest forward before my shoulders caught on either side of the duct. I loosely and ever so slightly bounced my knees, trying just to release some lactic acid from my sore muscles. They were starting to cramp up from being cooped up in such a small space.

What I wouldn't give to be outside running in the rain! Screw running and it could even be sunny and hot just so long as I made it back outside…again…someday.

I angrily swiped at a traitorous tear that snuck its way down my sweaty and dust smeared cheek. I shrugged my shoulders trying to relieve the onslaught of tension my thoughts had caused, opening and closing my fingers into tight fists and then stretching them open until they hurt. It had been several hours that I had been too afraid to take a deep breath, or make a sound let alone move. My eyes were adjusting to the lack of light coming through the filter.

They must have turned the lights off this time?

I was struggling trying to keep what was going on in my head and the terror that was happening all around me compartmentalized. I had to keep a grip on reality.

You've just got to hang on Rhea. Stay strong. You can do this.

Chapter
-12 Hours

"Rhea, yo' girlie. You've got to get the hell up!"

I groaned and rolled away from her pulling my covers up over my head.

"Oh hell no!" Emmory half laughed, half bitched as I felt her lunge onto the bed. Not even a second later she had straddled my back and was bouncing on me as though I were a trampoline or as though she were riding the mechanical bull at our favorite bar *'Pain & Aces'*. "It's a beautiful kind of pain, it's a beautiful kind of pain…find the light, find the light, find the light." Her voice was smooth, angelic and lyrical. I loved the notes that flowed from her soul and as a soul sister, she made mine twirl and dance at the sound of them.

I bucked her off recognizing the song that featured Emmory's favorite songwriter and vocalist. She patterned a lot of her musical choices, style and lyrics from a key handful of singers, and she was definitely one of them.

"Fuck Emm. I'm up already."

"Don't you get all A.M. high and mighty with me—it's not my fault that you stayed up so late."

"Oh come on!" Exasperated I tossed the covers back and threw my nicely shaped, smoothly shaven legs over the side of my futon bed. I knew Emmory and I were the perfect stereotypes for struggling musicians/community college students. She was your typical millennium-hippie, free-loving, folksy musician. I was pretty much the same, but less folksy and more Jennifer Aniston casual if you know what I mean. Other than our love of all things organic, natural, and homeopathic…and our intense partnership as vocalist and guitarist, we were opposites.

Emmory was tall for a girl at about 5'8". She was a curvy woman who enjoyed her spaghetti and liberally buttered sourdough bread more than she did her power-zumba classes. Her vibrant blonde waves framed an attractive, sun-kissed face. Her cheeks were round and her always smiling lips plump. She was from Europe somewhere, but with her skin so easily tanned to a golden hue—well, I had to wonder if one of the women in her lineage had had a sexy escapade with a Spaniard at one time or another.

Now on the other hand, well…let's just say that I was everything Emmory wasn't. Where she had the hour-glass curves, mine were understated. Boyish even. Where she came across as buxom and smiling, I was often described as plain and brooding. Perhaps that's why I had gotten more than my share of tattoos—to drive some interest my way? She was so damn sexy all the time, even as she fluctuated almost monthly from a size 10 to a 14 and back again…sometimes the other way around. The best part was that she just didn't give a shit.

Why can't I be more like that? Why do I say I don't care what people think, but do so much? A secret I'll hold to my grave.

My hair was a deep chestnut color that could even be described as black at times with brown highlights. Coming from Israeli decent; the second generation US born, meant that I was blessed with a trim athletic figure that I didn't have to work for—in spite of my love for running and swimming. And, I had *those* eyes. Not exactly the sexy ones that Arab women were getting in trouble with the religious police for having, but exotic enough that I could get away with little or no eye makeup and most people wouldn't know the difference. Where I did luck out if I do say so myself, was with the color of my eyes. They weren't just enticing, but they were nearly a clear blue. I caught men and women staring at me all the time, something that had made me self-conscious as a child and only recently grew to embrace.

I glanced at the clock on the vanity as I stepped out of the shower, feeling the pressure of the day weighing me down.

"Rhea? Hey—you really need to get a move on."

I cracked the door to let some cool air in to de-fog the mirror and came face to face with Emmory. "Hey, you can go on ahead—I can take my bike."

"Oh hun…you forgot? I have that demo to record in Portland today. There's just no way to have time to take you to PLCC and then make it back downtown by nine to make my appointment. You know how hard it was to get in."

"Yeah," I sighed heavily and shrugged halfheartedly. I had to admit I was envious as shit that she was making a demo without me, but they were using some prerecorded tracks as the background for her vocals. "I know. You'd better get a move on then." I smiled at her, trying my best to be encouraging. I looked her up and down and she looked every bit the rock star. I called after her as she turned and started down the hall, "You know Emm, you look stunning, really put together today. I just want you to know that. That's all." Perhaps it was the genuine infliction in my voice, or the sad look in my eyes that my act couldn't make up for but she came back towards me.

"You know, why don't you come? Yeah hun—I want you there. It would be great. Really. So, go get ready!" She waved her hands like a magician would expecting a trendy outfit to just magically appear on me. And, since we know that didn't happen I rushed past her and halted before my open bedroom door of our small college-esqe flat.

"Shit!" I spun around and leaned heavily into the wall. "I told my group that we'd meet after class to go over our presentation due next week on socio-economic status and its correlation to test scores. It's for my Economics 304 class." I cussed under my breath, "I'd better be there since I set it up. Damn. You go on ahead," I smiled. "But I want every detail of how cool it was when you get back okay? Promise me!"

She bounced over in her full-of-life way and gave me a brisk squeeze. "Sure thing Chickadee!" With that she turned, grabbed her old, tattered leather jacket and hemp shoulder bag off the hook by the door and the keys for her 1967 Royal Blue Ford Bronco and slammed the door behind her.

Damn, she's so cool.

I fucked around getting ready, my head just wasn't in the game. I was actually kicking myself for not going—it's not like anyone in my group would've been irreversibly bent out of shape by my rescheduling. But as part of my New Year's resolution to myself I was trying to be more responsible. Take my life more seriously instead of just coasting along—I was 21 after all. I glanced at myself in the heavy mahogany antique full-length mirror that hung by the door. It made everything reflected in it look beautiful, and how could it not? Its ornate wooden frame was one of a kind, carved by hand and given to my mom by her first and only true love—not, I feel compelled to mention, my dad. The reflection looking back at me made me smile for a second. I liked how my navy ruffled blouse sat at my hips and where my skinny jeans sat cuffed just above my ankles. I liked that my orange Chuck Norris Converse tennies pulled your attention down the length of my slender legs. My straight hair hung loosely and for once I looked fairly put together. I grabbed my green leather suede Lucky Brand boho bag, slung it over my shoulder and threw my backpack strap over my other shoulder. One final glance at the clock showed it was 7:50. There was no way I was going to make my first class in time.

Chapter
-11 Hours

8:10. I shook my head as I hastily walked to class. I had no idea how in the hell I had five minutes to spare. I walked into the College of Journalism and rushed into my Advanced Layout and Copywriting class, sliding into my wooden desk just as Isaac Matthews walked in. This was one class that I choose never to skip. Isaac Matthews was a Graduate Student, which meant—lucky for me, he was in his twenties. He was my morning tall blonde and sexy that I drank in along with my rolled oat and bran muffin. Okay, I obviously had a coffee too. I lived in the Pacific Northwest. Did anyone drink anything else? I was a creature of habit and had enjoyed this morning ritual most every morning as he'd taught the classes that I needed to graduate this year. I must have moaned my appreciation a bit louder than I'd intended as I caught a curious gaze out of the corner of my neighbor's eyes.

"Sorry," I whispered and received a gratuitous nod. Mr. Matthews after a short review, dove into his lecture on typeface and font-styles and their meanings for a good part of the hour. I shifted my legs, uncrossing and recrossing them.

Damn it!

I dropped my pen shuffling my notebook and laptop—yes, I still used both because I liked to draw and you just can't take those kinds of notes on your computer. I reached down to retrieve it and noticed leather flip-flops standing in the aisle beside me.

"Ms. Kenzee?"

Oh Crap! What the fuck did he just ask me?

"I'm sorry, Mr. Matthews. I didn't hear what you'd asked me. Could you please repeat it?" I smiled up at him sheepishly.

Oh come on! It's not like I am the only girl in here with a crush on you. Lighten up?

He smiled down at me. "I would, Ms. Kenzee but I haven't asked you yet."

"Oh." All I could do was nod at him like an idiot.

"We were discussing fonts that were used for the MontBlanc Fountain Pen ad campaign and I'm asking you now specifically—what font you would use for a Time Square billboard and why." He smiled down at me and cocked an eyebrow.

"I, I…well, off the top of my head I would use Segoe Script or Mistral."

Isaac Matthews cleared his throat and cocked his head ever so slightly like a dog who was puzzled by his master. "And why Ms. Kenzee would those be your choices? MontBlanc is one of the finest, most luxurious pen companies in the world. Most students in this class—nay in any advertising design and layout class would have gone with a script like French or Freestyle."

"While that may be so, Mr. Matthews," I paused and sucked in a deep breath, "I'm not like most students. I feel the targeted audience for the campaign—the pompous, overindulged, powerfully reckless businessman would appreciate the strength of the lines and the power in those fonts." My head whipped to the door separating us from the commotion that was going on outside in the hallway. Isaac turned at that same time and in several lithe strides was back down the wooden stairs of the tiered classroom and out the main door. Seconds later he reentered.

"Alright, everyone up. Take your things—it appears we have a drill of some sort. Meet on the Annex lawn to be accounted for." He shook his head and then called out, "Ms. Kenzee, a moment please."

I lifted my head in puzzlement, but continued to pack up my gear. I stood so the row could get past me, then squatted back down to finish compiling everything. Some idiot had snagged my purse with his boot and the contents had scattered all over the floor. And then I felt a presence, someone close. I heard the classroom door bang shut with finality. Closed-off from the riot outside in the hallway. Inside, there wasn't a single sound.

"Rhea?"

I glanced up and the wind was taken from my sails. Isaac Matthews was…well, to put it simply. He was beautiful. Not in the whole big man on campus way or even because he was so well built, but more in a nerdy intellectual way. I was drawn to him and I couldn't fathom why outside of his good-looks, brains… Fuck! Who was I kidding he just had a certain Je-ne-sais-quoi. An inexpressible something that drew me to him and from the look in his eyes, he felt it too. It wasn't like it was anything that we'd ever be able to explore. After all I was a senior and he was a graduate student and his Stahlen Fellowship would be at serious risk if he did.

"Rhea, I just wanted to express my sincerest appreciation for what you bring to this lecture. When you said that you weren't like most students, which was one of the truest statements that I've heard in a long while, I couldn't have agreed more. I like that you challenge conventional thinking and I just wanted you to know that I've identified you as a PLCC Academic Shooting Star."

I felt dumb-struck and a little start-struck too. His pheromones were getting to me—he smelled so, soo good. "Mr. Matthe…"

"I'd prefer you call me Isaac when it's just the two of us. After all, we won't always be confined by the teacher/student parameters."

Did he just say what I think he said? Did he just allude to the future—one with him and I in it together? As in together-together? No fucking way?!

JUST THEN, A SHOT RANG OUT.

Chapter
-10 Hours

Isaac's eyes only seconds before were warm and inviting, now they were full of panic and fear. He grabbed my hand and jerked me up. I glanced up at the large institutional clock that hung above the door. 9:05, before I snatched my purse off the floor where I had been reassembling it. He strode to the back of the classroom in intentional strides that were driven by fear and adrenaline, then stopped. There in front of us, in the corner of the room was a two foot by three foot screened air vent. He knelt and with his thumb pushed on the spring-release screws in the vent's corners until they gave—freeing the vent. A black hole was revealed.

"Get in."

I just looked at Isaac and then to the door and back to him. "I, I don't know if I can get in there. It's so…dark."

A SHOT RANG OUT…CLOSER THIS TIME.

"Rhea, Jeezus! Get in! Hurry!"

I was so scared, so panicked that time had ceased to exist. I could hear screaming and men's voices yelling. If I had had my wits about me I could've discerned that the gunmen were sweeping the classrooms. It would've registered that if they were close enough for me to hear, it wouldn't be long before they were here. Isaac embraced me in a full-bodied hug and his lips came down on mine in a soft, gentle kiss. It wasn't searching at all. It was goodbye.

"Rhea, please?!" he begged urgently.

I nodded and looked into his eyes before sitting in the back hole. No sooner had I pulled my feet in had he placed the vent screen back in place and was screwing it in.

"Isaac!" My voice called out in a shaky whisper. It was choked and not nearly as loud as I had intended it to be. "Where are you going?"

"Don't worry about me. I'll hide in the attic access down the hall. Just don't say a word. Don't breathe. These guys mean business…and for God's sake, make sure your phone's volume is off."

"Isaac, I'm…I'm just so scared…" Tears now ran down my cheeks.

"Just pray. They shouldn't find you here. I've got to go." I heard him stand up and move to the rear door of the classroom and down the stairs. I heard the door handle turn and I could only assume that he was checking out the hallway. I didn't hear any voices. That was a good sign. Then the door quietly clicked closed.

Isaac was gone.

I was all alone.

I was operating in near total darkness as the vent didn't let very much light in. There was no way that I could continue to sit here in this duct in the position that I was in, so I carefully slid myself backward, as much as I hated to leave the comfort the sparse light created. I only had to slide back about four feet before my back hit the 'T' in the ductwork. I paused.

There was silence. Nobody had come into the classroom yet. I dug in the dark, searching through my purse in search of my phone. As my fingers closed around their treasure, I heard the classroom door bang open. I froze. I stopped breathing. Was it Isaac saying everything was okay?

Holy Fuck! Was that a…?

THEN A THIRD SHOT RANG OUT.

Voices got angrier and louder as they burst into the classroom. I explored my surroundings and to my left felt a dead-end in the ductwork. I drew my knees up to my chest, pulling my legs out of the duct that led to the vent—my only protection from THEM, and scooted myself back into the end-piece. If I drew my legs all the way up to my chest, only my toes would be visible from the vent, and cloaked in the oppressive, thick, inky-darkness, probably not at all. I took my first deep breath in I don't know how long. For the briefest of seconds I felt the smidge of optimism that they just might *not* find me. I might just come out of this okay.

"All you fuckers listen up. Jaybird and Wishbone have the students and teachers we found on this floor corralled in a large lecture hall downstairs. I haven't gotten word from Jester and Boom if their team's secured the top two floors."

I heard a loud bang and some muffled arguing.

"I don't give a shit what you think Crush, it's what needed to be done!"

I could hear the low, angry growl sparring with a quieter although just as impassioned voice and made out the words 'kill' and 'just kids'. I scooted forward just a tad so that I had a better chance of hearing what was going on. Clearly the ring-leader was trying to squelch a rebellious gang-member. With my head closer to the vent, I could better make out what they were saying.

"Mercy, I understand you're point, but man. I didn't sign up for this!" The nervous tone in his voice was palpable. "You just said that we'd move in and sweep. You know," and I heard movement and assumed it was him. "THAT fucker didn't have the right to open fire."

"Who are you calling fucker?" The voice was low, a sinister growl. The same voice as before. "I did what I needed to do to get them downstairs. These privileged punks weren't listening to us; they acted like these fucking guns were props or they were in a fucking movie or something. And that stupid fucking bitch, she stuck her nose up at me and taunted me to shoot her, said she wasn't going anywhere. I had to show them we meant business."

It was the voice of reason that spoke again. "I don't give a shit, Mercy, what Spider said his reasoning was. I'm out."

There was more commotion and it sounded like someone was slammed into a door or wall. It amazed me that with my sight all but paralyzed, my hearing became more acute. So did my ability to provide logical explanations for what I was hearing.

"No-fucking-body is OUT! You got me? I told all of you dumbshits that once you were in, you were in. You knew what you signed on for. You couldn't have been so fucking stupid to think that it couldn't come to this. If you're out, it will be the fourth bullet of the day in the head that takes you out. Is that fucking clear?" He paused and I felt for the poor boy who had had a change of heart. "Crush! Is that fucking clear?"

"Y…y…yes. Yes Mercy. Crystal." He stammered and that low, threatening voice mocked him, mimicking his stutter.

That voice. What's his name? Wasn't it something like…Spider! His name is Spider. Keep track Rhea. You have to keep track of who they are.

The gang on the other side of my vent seemed to have calmed down some, so their voices didn't carry enough for me to catch much of the conversation. I slid my butt back until it met the end-portion of the duct and pulled my purse back onto my lap. Man was I glad I'd grabbed it.

Fuck! My backpack. I left it in there. It has my planner, my thumb-drive…they'll be able to find out who I am and where I live.

MY WALLET. I'd crammed it into the front pocket after I'd gotten my coffee, now it was in my backpack…in the classroom. *I am so, SO screwed.*

I reached into my purse and turned my phone on. I was hoping that with it staying in my purse, the suede would block out any light from it. It powered out of its sleep mode with an intensely bright white light. I folded my purse over so that no more light could escape.

Fuck! Please tell me that they couldn't see that!

I reopened my purse just a little, and bent my head closer to it, trying as hard as I could to contain the screen's bright light. I scrolled through my contacts stopping on Emmory's number. I tapped the compose message icon.

> EMMORY,
> CONTACT THE POLICE.
> THE COLLEGE IS UNDER ATTACK.
> I DON'T KNOW IF IT IS THE WHOLE CAMPUS OR JUST THE SCHOOL OF JOURNALISM BUT GUNMEN HAVE TAKEN CONTROL. THE RING LEADER'S NAME IS MERCY. JAYBIRD AND ONE OTHER ARE HOLDING STUDENTS AND TEACHERS IMPRISIONED IN A LECTURE HALL ON THE FIRST FLOOR. MERCY, SPIDER AND CRUSH ARE ON THE SECOND FLOOR. I DON'T KNOW HOW MANY MORE, BUT THERE ARE TWO LEADERS ON THE TOP TWO FLOORS AND THEY HAVE A TEAM TOO. MR. MATTHEWS IS IN THE ATTIC. I AM HIDING.

GET HELP.
THERE ARE AT LEAST THREE
SHOTS FIRED WITH FATALITIES.
~RHEA~

I hit send. My phone beeped. I slammed my purse closed again and strained to hear THEIR voices. I figured if I heard voices, then they couldn't have heard me.

SILENCE.

I sat in the thick blackness, its weight crushing the air from my lungs. I drew in only enough air to keep me alive. After a pause that seemed like an eternity, I heard muted voices coming from down in front of the classroom. The air rushed out of my lungs in a subconscious gust of relief.

I dug back into my purse and staring me in the face: MESSAGE NOT SENT glared back at me. That message crushed me more than I would have ever imagined.

What the fuck now? Now what do I do? Dear Father, Lord in Heaven...please, PLEASE get me out of this. Get us all out of this. Please God.

I changed all of my phone's volume settings and turned it off. I sat in the oppressive blackness for minutes, time standing still and yet moving me ever closer to the final ending.

Chapter
-9 Hours

My phone screen blinked on. 10:12. Had this really been going on for over an hour already? A blinking blue light on my phone finally caught my attention. I'd been sitting, staring down the long duct in front of me. My eyes had adjusted to the dark and the meager light that was filtering in through the heating and air conditioning vent. I could see that I was inside a formidable air duct that ended where I was sitting, 'T'-ed at the classroom I'd been in, and then continued down a long ways. Small arcs of dim light made their way to this main duct and I knew at those points, there were vents that led to other classrooms.

I glanced back at my phone and swiped to unlock my screen. My notifications showed that I had received an email.

An email? How could I have gotten an email if my text wasn't sent?

I had spent the last several minutes trying to rationalize why my text hadn't been sent and all I could come up with was that the gunmen had a jammer on—keeping anyone, and all of us from communicating with the outside world. So then why or rather, how could I have gotten an email?

I touched my email icon and sure enough I had received an email from someone in my afternoon Copywriting class.

SUBJECT: YOU ARE NOT ALONE
TO:
RheaVelvetKenzee@pacificlakescommunityc
ollege.us.net

FROM: EliValenSnohe@pacificlakescommunitycollege.us.net

RHEA,

THIS IS ELI SNOHE. I AM SENDING THIS MESSAGE OUT TO PROFESSOR DUNCAN'S ADVANCED COPYWRITING CLASS LIST. I NEED TO KNOW IF I AM ALONE. ARE YOU SAFE? DO THEY HAVE YOU? I JUST WANTED YOU TO KNOW YOU ARE NOT ALONE.

ELI

How could he be emailing me? Do they have him? I set to work emailing him right back.

SUBJECT: RE: YOU ARE NOT ALONE

TO: EliValenSnohe@pacificlakescommunitycollege.us.net

FROM: RheaVelvetKenzee@pacificlakescommunitycollege.us.net

ELI,

I AM AS FINE AS I CAN BE UNDER THE CIRCUMSTANCES. HOW ARE YOU? ARE YOU HIDING SOMEWHERE? ARE YOU SAFE? AND BTW, HOW ARE WE EMAILING IF PHONE TEXTS WON'T GO THROUGH? I HAD FIGURED THE GUNMEN HAD JAMMED THE SIGNAL.

~RHEA~

Outside the vent the group's conversation had gotten heated again. I swiped at a bead of sweat and wished like hell someone could've change the heating controls before I was crammed up in the duct work. I felt like I was baking.

"Damn it! Damn it! Damn it!" Something hit the wall and I could only imagine the gunman bitching was the one who had thrown something.

"Calm the fuck down. The police never acquiesce to any perpetrator's first request. We'll get what we want or they'll have a huge fucking mess to clean up!"

I slid back into my cubby alcove and slumped against the wall. *How could they be doing this to all of us, and why?* The flashing blue light indicated that Eli had already gotten back to me. I swiped the screen and opened the newest email.

SUBJECT: JUST BREATHE, WE'VE GOT THIS

TO: RheaVelvetKenzee@pacificlakescommunitycollege.us.net

FROM: EliValenSnohe@pacificlakescommunitycollege.us.net

RHEA,

I AM HIDING AS I ASSUME YOU ARE TOO. NOBODY FROM THE CLASS LIST HAS GOTTEN BACK TO ME YET EXCEPT YOU. I DO HOPE THAT SOMEONE IS OFF CAMPUS AND WILL CHECK THEIR EMAIL BEFORE COMING TO CLASS. I AM NOT SURE WHY WE

CAN EMAIL, BUT AFTER SOME
THOUGHT I'VE COME TO THE
CONCLUSION THAT IT MUST BE
BECAUSE THEY PLACED A JAMMER
SIGNAL. YOU ARE ABLE TO ACCESS
THE SCHOOL'S EMAIL BECAUSE YOU
ARE USING THE WIFI AS A GUEST OFF
THE ROOM NEXT TO, ABOVE, OR
BELOW YOU. I AM NOT A TECH, BUT
THERE HAS TO BE SOME REASON
THAT THE SCHOOL EMAIL WORKS
AND NOTHING ELSE DOES. MAYBE A
DIFFERENT NETWORK OR
MAINFRAME OR SOMETHING?
ELI.

Well, he was right. I'd give him that. Who really cared anyways how it all worked, I was just glad that I wasn't completely alone. I copied the text that I had sent Emmory, to Eli and hit send. That way, he'd at least know the details that I had pieced together. Then I went to work sending out an email to Emmory using her school account.

SUBJECT: CALL THE POLICE,
WE'RE HELD HOSTAGE
TO:
EmmoryVanessaJane@pacificlakescommunitycollege.us.net
FROM:
RheaVelvetKenzee@pacificlakescommunitycollege.us.net
EMMORY,
CONTACT THE POLICE.

THE COLLEGE IS UNDER
ATTACK IN CASE YOU DIDN'T
ALREADY KNOW…FIRST SHOT FIRED
JUST AFTER 9:00.
          THERE ARE IN EXCESS OF
EIGHT GUNMEN THAT I'VE COUNTED
SO FAR, THREE IN THE ROOM NEXT TO
ME, TWO DOWNSTAIRS AND AT LEAST
THREE UPSTAIRS TOO. I AM HIDING.
GET HELP. THERE ARE AT LEAST
THREE SHOTS FIRED WITH
FATALITIES.
          ~RHEA~

I hit send and crossed my fingers that she'd see it. I arched my back trying to get as good of a stretch in as I could, but let's face it—when you're stuck in an air duct that's maybe three feet high by two feet wide, there just wasn't the space to get comfortable. Not, that under the circumstances I could even begin to anyways. I gently jounced my knees working the cramps out of them, when suddenly, my heart slammed into my chest.

"Hey Mercy! Come take a look at this!"

The voice of reason—Crush—was entirely too close to the vent for my liking. Now I was wishing that I'd sat closer to the front of the classroom…then he wouldn't be all up in my safety zone. I figured he was only maybe twelve or fifteen feet from my vent.

Oh God why do I like to sit in one of the last two rows?

I was giving myself grief when a voice, that low menacing growl of a voice did stop my heart.

"Oh yeah? What the fuck did the wee-little man find, besides his conscience?"

The voice came from what sounded like right outside the vent. I was too afraid to pull my legs in for any sound at all would alert him to where I was, and yet I felt too exposed, as though he could see me already. I started feeling light headed.

Breathe Rhea, take a breath…

I slowly drew my legs into my chest as I drew in a breath at the same time and none too soon either.

"Hey, did you fuckers see this vent?" I could hear him hitting the vent. Smacking it real good.

I DIDN'T DARE BREATHE.

I pulled my legs in even farther, I doubt if even my toes showed past the end-portion now.

"Mercy man, bring me your gun. I want to use the light on it to shine it in this vent. I don't know why, but I just have a feeling."

Oh my God. Oh my God. Oh my God.

It was taking every single cell in my body to hold still, every ounce of strength that I possessed to not make a sound. The fear in me radiated from every pore and I was strung taught like a rubber band that was ready to snap. All I could do was pray.

"I don't give a fuck if it's closed tight. Bring me the goddamn light!"

I could hear movement down in front of the classroom, and simultaneously sounds that indicated that Spider, the owner of that menacing voice had knelt down in front of the vent. My pulse accelerated proportionately to each step as I heard the heavy weight of boots ascending the wooden stairs.

"Fucker, you took long enough!" I heard a dull thud followed by the sound of a body hitting the floor.

"You'd better remember who's in charge. I never have taken shit from nobody and don't plan to start now." Mercy's voice was enraged, controlled and he meant business. The cool rage that he directed toward Spider gave me chills. My body was covered in goosebumps in spite of being covered in sweat and the heat pumping through the ducts. "Let me ask you this, you low life piece of shit. Where would you be right now if it weren't for me? WHERE?!"

"Nowhere, Boss."

"That's right. Without me you'd have no cause, you'd have no life, you'd have no purpose. Don't you forget that."

"Yes, Boss."

"Good. Now forget about that vent. It's sealed up real tight—you pounded on it right?"

"Yes, Boss."

"Did it wiggle or come loose?"

"No. Boss."

"Alright then. Take Crush and go see what is going on downstairs. I want you to speak with Jester and Boom, then get a detailed report for me on the top two floors. Got it?"

"Yes, Boss."

"And no more fighting with each other, it'll take all of us to pull this off."

I took in a breath of fresh air, rolled my neck and stretched my legs out the moment I heard Spider get up and move down the stairs. Some muted arguing indicated that he had met up with Crush and soon after the door closed. But, where was Mercy at?

Holy Hell! What the fuck was that? Is he right here?

Again, I pulled my legs ever so slowly back into my chest and found that I had stopped breathing. I only took in the smallest breath of air—just enough so that I didn't pass out. And it was none too soon. A piercing bright light drove into the darkness through the vent grate. I pulled my legs even farther into my body—if that were even possible.

He can see my toes. I KNOW he can see my toes. Oh my God! Where's my purse?

My eyes jetted out to the few feet in front of me and sure enough—there my green suede purse sat.

Oh my God...NO!

"What the hell?" I heard him mutter to himself and the light disappeared. I heard heavy boots descending the steps. I took this few seconds to pull my purse…dragging it slowly and silently into my hidden space, tucking it into my butt so that it was no longer visible.

Then, I heard him climb the steps again. He stopped in front of the vent and dropped to his knees. I heard him grunting as he was either bending over or laying prone…I wasn't sure which, but how he was laying mattered less to me as soon as a spotlight flashlight-type was shone in through the vent.

"Okay, where are you?" I heard him muttering to himself in a strained voice. He had to be on his belly. I squeezed my eyes tightly shut and grabbed my knees for dear life. I was afraid he'd hear my watch ticking, my knees knocking, the beat of my heart; hell, I was for sure he could hear the blood rushing in my ears and my breathing. So, I stopped.

He shone the spotlight beam all around, the side of the light-beam hitting my toes a few times and the back wall of the vent next to my thigh. I had drawn myself back as much as I possibly could and now could do nothing more than believe in prayer and hope for the best. A few seconds passed, a minute maybe, but in my world it felt like forever. Each second felt like the difference between life and death. I now knew what it felt like to be the prey; cuddled up, helpless and at the mercy of a predator.

Finally, the light left me.

Alone.

Scared.

Immersed in dark.

Chapter
-8 Hours

Mercy was clever. He was the cat and I was the mouse. He lay in waiting several minutes, and at sporadic intervals would blast me with the light—blinding me. Terrifying me. Each time nearly stopping my heart. But each time I lucked out. Somehow he never discovered me. At long last I heard him grunt as he stood up and stalk off heavily down the classroom stairs. The door first opened then closed.

Am I alone?

I felt my phone vibrate and glanced into my purse, the screen read 11:22. Had it really only been two hours? I was exhausted and weak from the onslaught my body had taken from all the adrenaline that had slammed into my veins every time I'd had a scare. When would this end; when everyone was dead? When the cops came? When they gave the gunmen what they wanted?

A SHOT RANG OUT.

My body froze. Its ability to respond now to terror was astounding.

That's number four. What do these guys want with us?

In spite of my best efforts, a barrage of tears erupted and I wept silently. It felt good, it was cathartic. I'd need that release and never would've allowed it had my body not just taken over and done what it needed. I'd have to thank it later—if I made it out of here alive.

Stop it right now! Stop acting like no one's going to make it out alive. I'm hidden, Eli's hidden...who knows how many more are hidden. The police will come, they'll save us.

I sat in the dark unknowingly nodding to myself, convincing myself that despite the facts that stacked up against our getting out of this alive, we *would* make it out of here.

THE PHONE! I'd nearly forgotten that I'd seen the blue light blinking—an indication that I'd received either a text or an email. I quickly dug into my purse, excited to see who had gotten back to me. My fingers wrapped around it and I swiped at the screen pulling up my emails. *Yes! There are TWO!*

I rolled my neck easing the tension from my muscles, extended my legs while bouncing my knees, and rotated my ankles. I couldn't believe how excited I was about seeing who had contacted me. It was as though I were sitting down in my deep leather chair with my favorite minky blanket, my all-time favorite book and a warm cup of Seattle's Best. I laughed to myself.

You're definitely losing it girl!

SUBJECT: JUST KEEPING IT REAL

TO: RheaVelvetKenzee@pacificlakescommunitycollege.us.net

FROM: EliValenSnohe@pacificlakescommunitycollege.us.net

RHEA,

YOU KNOW, I AM NOT TOO SURE WHAT TO SAY. I BOUNCE BETWEEN FEELING ALL ALONE AND REALIZING THAT YOU ARE IN THIS WITH ME. I GUESS THE GOOD NEWS IS THAT THE AD PROOF WE HAD DUE TODAY…WELL, I BET WE CAN GET AN EXTENSION ON IT. HAHA

I AM SITTING HERE IN THE DARK, SEQUESTERED AWAY WITH ONLY MY TABLET AND PRAY THE BATTERY LASTS ME LONGER THAN THIS WHOLE ORDEAL.

WHY DO YOU SUPPOSE THEY ARE DOING THIS? WHAT IS THEIR MOTIVE? THAT'S WHAT I KEEP COMING BACK TO. THANKS FOR THE INFORMATION EARLIER. I DIDN'T KNOW WHO OR HOW MANY WE ARE DEALING WITH. YOU MUST BE RIGHT THERE IN IT DEEP HUH?

WELL, SO ANYWAYS I FIGURED SINCE NEITHER OF US HAS ANYTHING BETTER TO DO, IT WOULDN'T HURT TO SAY 'HI' AND INTRODUCE MYSELF. HAHA.

SO ANYWAYS, IN CASE YOU HADN'T NOTICED, I'M ONE OF THE…LIKE TEN GUYS IN OUR CLASS WITH DARK HAIR, ONE OF LIKE…FIVE OF THOSE GUYS WITH A SORRY EXCUSE FOR FACIAL HAIR. HELL, WHO AM I KIDDING? IT'S MORE LIKE A FIVE-O'CLOCK SHADOW THAT JUST WON'T GROW IN.

MAN, AM I EVEN MAKING ANY SENSE? SOMEHOW TALKING TO YOU MAKES ME FEEL LESS ALONE. I'M PRAYING FOR YOU AND HOPE YOU'RE OKAY.

ELI.

Wow. I really wasn't alone, and it was so reassuring that there was someone else who was going through the exact same thing as I was, who could emphasize with what I was feeling. Shit, he was probably even feeling the same things I was. It was nice to feel myself relax just the smallest amount while I read his note and I'd even found myself smiling.

Wow! What's with that?

I quickly set about opening my second email.

SUBJECT: WHY WON'T YOU ANSWER ME?

TO: RheaVelvetKenzee@pacificlakescommunitycollege.us.net

FROM: EliValenSnohe@pacificlakescommunitycollege.us.net

RHEA,

I HAVEN'T HEARD BACK FROM YOU AND I'M WORRIED. FUCK, IT'S MORE LIKE I'M SCARED SHITLESS. WHERE ARE YOU? YOU'D BETTER BE OKAY!

ELI.

Again, I caught myself smiling. More tension eased from my shoulders. I stretched my fingers and began to type.

SUBJECT: SLOW YOUR ROLL!

I'M FINE ☺

TO:
EliValenSnohe@pacificlakescommunitycollege.us.net
FROM:
RheaVelvetKenzee@pacificlakescommunitycollege.us.net
ELI,
I AM ALIVE AND KICKING. IT GOT PRETTY HAIRY THERE FOR AWHILE, THE MAIN BOSS 'MERCY' WAS SHINING A LIGHT IN MY HIDEY-HOLE. I VERY NEARLY CRAPPED MY PANTS. J/K. NO, BUT REALLY I ABOUT SUFFERED A HEART ATTACK AND HAD TO REMIND MYSELF TO BREATHE. AT LEAST NOW THAT HE'S LOOKED HERE, HE PROBABLY WON'T AGAIN. AT LEAST THAT'S SOMETHING TO BE THANKFUL FOR.

AS FAR AS OUR ASSIGNMENT GOES…OH CRAP! CAN YOU BELIEVE THAT I FORGOT? I SKETCHED IT OUT, WORKED ON THE COPY…BUT NEVER FINISHED MY PROOF. MAYBE I AM GLAD THIS ALL HAPPENED AFTERALL. HAHA. BIG J/K!!

SO AS FAR AS WHO YOU ARE…I BET YOU'RE NOT SURPRISED THAT YOU DIDN'T NARROW IT DOWN ENOUGH FOR ME, BUT DON'T FEEL TOO BADLY OUR CLASS HAS WHAT…SIXTY OR SO STUDENTS IN IT? BTW, EVERYONE SEEMS TO BE

GROWING A BEARD, SO THAT TIDBIT DIDN'T HELP. LOL

IF YOU WERE THE ONLY ONE WITHOUT ONE…MAYBE THEN I'D KNOW WHO YOU WERE. NAH, PROBABLY NOT. I'M NOT THAT OBSERVANT. HAHA

WOW. THIS IS GETTING REALLY LONG. I HAD NO IDEA I WAS SO LONG-WINDED.

SO, IT SEEMS LIKE YOU KNOW WHO I AM. I'D TRY TO DESCRIBE MYSELF BY TELLING YOU ABOUT MY MOUSEY BROWN HAIR OR THAT I'M LIKE 5'4 AND 110, BUT I'D BET THAT WOULDN'T NARROW ME DOWN. WHAT MIGHT HELP IS IF I TELL YOU I'M THE ONE WITH CLEAR BLUE EYES. IT SEEMS THAT IS SOMETHING EVERYONE NOTICES. WELL, I HOPE THAT HELPS.

BTW, I REALLY LIKE THE NAME ELI AND HOW UNUSUAL VALEN IS.
~RHEA~

I hit send and shifted my weight. Lately, say the last thirty or forty minutes or so, no matter how I moved or where I put my ass, my legs fell asleep. I slumped down a bit more searching for any position that would lessen the numbness in them. So far, it wasn't working.

I stopped moving, thinking that maybe someone had entered the room, but only silence greeted me. I was beyond relieved. I sat in the darkness just thinking. I thought about what if I continued having to stay hidden? I'd need to find a vending machine and at the very least a bathroom. I had a pretty good idea the ductwork's layout and could guess where at least the first few vents up ahead went to. I was hoping that there was a 'T' up ahead that paralleled the hallway that ran just outside this classroom. If there was, then I'd know exactly where the bathroom was.

I ran my hands along the ridged metal walls I was wedged between hoisting myself forward in small increments until I had the hip room to flip myself over. Once on my stomach, I pushed myself farther down the duct, stopping when my shoulders lined up with the corners of the 'T'. I laid on my side with my head facing the vent, staring out of it, and the light that it let through with the leaves dancing in it—well, it created beautiful shadows that had me feeling like I was watching late-night TV's shadows as they played on my living room wall. My eyes began to glaze and exhaustion threatened to overtake me.

Yay! My phone just vibrated. Whoo Hoo! I hope it's Eli.

I slid farther down the long-side of the duct until my head was completely cloaked in darkness. I wanted to make sure that if Mercy or that other asshole Spider shone their lights through the vent again, that I was in no way visible. I pulled my phone out of the back pocket I had shoved it in before I changed positions and turned it on and swiped the screen all in one movement. I rolled onto my back and found myself getting mentally comfortable—hell, a smile had already shown up on my face and I hadn't even confirmed the email was from Eli.

BooYa! I'm in the money…Whoo Hoo!

There looking at me was not one, not two, but three emails. I clicked on the first.

SUBJECT: WHAT A SHITTY FUCKING ATTEMPT
TO: RheaVelvetKenzee@pacificlakescommunitycollege.us.net
FROM: EmmoryVanessaJane@pacificlakescommunitycollege.us.net
NEED A LITTLE ATTENTION RHEA?
I THINK IT IS PRETTY BULLSHIT TO SEND ME A MESSAGE LIKE THAT WHILE I AM HERE ON ONE OF THE BIGGEST DAYS OF MY LIFE, MAKING THE RECORDING THAT I'VE ALWAYS DREAMT OF MAKING.
I EXTENDED AN INVITATION TO YOU THIS MORNING. I NEVER FIGURED YOU FOR THE JEALOUS TYPE.
GROW UP!
AND BTW, GO *FUCK* YOURSELF.
*EMM

My mouth hung open in total and utter shock. Emmory didn't believe me? How could she *not* believe me…I had never given her any reason not to. The part of the email that wrecked me the most, was finding out that she had such a low opinion of me. She thought I could be petty and jealous, *and* intentionally mean. I mean, REALLY? How is it that I didn't already know this about her after living with her since our freshman year? I clicked reply before I could stop myself.

SUBJECT: CONTACT THE POLICE. NOW! YOU BITCH!

TO: EmmoryVanessaJane@pacificlakescommunitycollege.us.net

FROM: RheaVelvetKenzee@pacificlakescommunitycollege.us.net

THE ONLY, AND I MEAN *ONLY* REASON THAT I DON'T HATE YOU FOR SAYING THOSE THINGS IS BECAUSE I NEED FOR YOU TO CALL THE POLICE.

GIVE THEM THE DETAILS THAT I GAVE YOU IN THE EARLIER EMAIL BUT TELL THEM THERE'S BEEN FOUR SHOTS FIRED, NOT THREE LIKE I HAD INDICATED EARLIER.

~RHEA~

God, her email had totally ruined my mood. She was my best-friend, the yin to my yang, the salt to my pepper. I mean, she was the lyricist to my melodies. Fuck! Why'd she have to go and mess up such a good thing? I mean we're sisters.

My eyes glistened with unshed tears and I rolled on my side facing away from the light. I glanced at the time on my homepage. 12:08.

Chapter
-6 Hours

My eyes flew open at the sound of voices in the room next to me. I shielded my phone from the vent and checked for notifications. I had six.

Oh fuck! Eli! I forgot to get back to him before I nodded off.

My phone read 1:17. Thank God, I was only out for about an hour, it wouldn't be too hard for me to figure out what was going in the room next door…would it? I turned my phone off deciding that I needed to try to figure out what was going on so that I could really enjoy my messages. After stashing my phone in my rear pocket, I carefully, and very quietly pushed up onto all fours as best as the duct would allow. I walked my hands and knees forward all the while making sure that the voices I heard just kept right on talking. I did my 180 shift so that I found myself back on my ass, and scooted it back into my little dead-end cubby hole. I listened to the voices sparring and throwing insults, but none of it actually made me say hmm.

So, I focused my attention on my emails. I whipped out my phone that I had forgotten about and was now sitting on, turned it on and swiped the screen. EIGHT emails!?

SUBJECT: WHY WON'T YOU ANSWER ME?

TO: RheaVelvetKenzee@pacificlakescommunitycollege.us.net

FROM: EliValenSnohe@pacificlakescommunitycollege.us.net

RHEA,

I LIKE THAT YOU'RE LONG WINDED. I REALLY LIKE HEARING WHAT YOU HAVE TO SAY. YOU MAKE ME SMILE. GOD, CAN I EVEN SAY THAT WITHOUT SOUNDING LIKE A DAMN PERVERT? WELL, JUST KNOW I DIDN'T MEAN ANYTHING FROM IT AND I KNOW WE JUST STARTED TALKING, BUT YOU MAKE ME FEEL LIKE ALL THIS ISN'T GOING ON WHEN I READ YOUR EMAIL.

ENOUGH OF THAT. YOU'LL FIND THAT THE MORE I TALK, THE WORSE I TEND TO MAKE THINGS.

I MEAN, I HOPE YOU GET THE CHANCE TO FIND THAT OUT.

I'M GLAD YOU LIKE MY NAME. MY PARENTS CHOOSE ELI, WELL…AS THE STORY GOES, THEY WANTED A STRONG NAME. IT MEANS DEFENDER OF MAN, THE HIGH AND ASCENDED OR 'MY GOD'.

YOU MENTIONED VALEN, AND YOU'RE RIGHT IT IS UNCOMMON. IT IS LATIN AND MEANS 'STRONG'. HAHA, I DID TELL YOU THAT THEY WANTED A NAME THAT WAS A STRONG ONE.

ENOUGH ABOUT ME.

SO SORRY TO HEAR YOU HAD SUCH A SCARY EXPERIENCE, BUT I'M SURE YOU'RE RIGHT THAT THEY WON'T LOOK FOR YOU AGAIN. I'M

GLAD YOU'RE OKAY…BUT WONDER IF YOU REALLY ARE?
ELI.
BTW, I KNOW EXACTLY WHO YOU ARE. I KNEW EVEN BEFORE YOU TOLD ME ABOUT YOUR EYES. ☺

Still smiling, I clicked on the next email.

SUBJECT: RHEA?
TO: RheaVelvetKenzee@pacificlakescommunitycollege.us.net
FROM: EliValenSnohe@pacificlakescommunitycollege.us.net
RHEA,
I HAVEN'T HEARD BACK FROM YOU AND I'M REALLY STARTING TO WORRY.
ELI.

SUBJECT: JEEZUS, WHERE ARE YOU?
TO: RheaVelvetKenzee@pacificlakescommunitycollege.us.net
FROM: EliValenSnohe@pacificlakescommunitycollege.us.net
RHEA,
I KNOW I SHOULDN'T PANIC CAUSE YOU SAID YOU WERE WELL

HIDDEN, BUT HOW CAN I NOT? I
HAVEN'T SMILED IN OVER AN HOUR.
WHERE COULD YOU BE?
ELI.

SUBJECT: JUST LET ME KNOW
YOU'RE OKAY
TO:
RheaVelvetKenzee@pacificlakescommunityc
ollege.us.net
FROM:
EliValenSnohe@pacificlakescommunitycolle
ge.us.net
PLEASE JUST LET ME KNOW
YOU'RE OKAY RHEA VELVET.
ELI.
P.S. HOW'D YOUR PARENTS COME UP
WITH YOUR NAME? I'VE BEEN
WONDERING AS THER ISN'T TOO
MUCH ELSE TO WONDER ABOUT.

SUBJECT: REALLY, I'M NOT A
CRAZY STALKER PERSON
TO:
RheaVelvetKenzee@pacificlakescommunityc
ollege.us.net
FROM:
EliValenSnohe@pacificlakescommunitycolle
ge.us.net
RHEA,
RATIONAL THOUGHT TELLS ME
THAT YOU'RE OKAY, BUT MY
EMOTIONAL SIDE IS WORRIED.

PLEASE EMAIL ME WHEN YOU GET THIS. I REALLY HOPE THAT I AM NOT COMING OFF AS A WEIRDO—REALLY, I AM *NOT* NORMALLY THIS…WELL, ANYTHING. I NEVER WIGOUT LIKE THIS ON ANYONE. PLEASE JUST KNOW IT IS THE SITUATION WE'RE IN. I SEE YOU AS KIND OF THE ONLY OTHER PERSON IN THIS WITH ME.

ANYWAYS, I WON'T EMAIL YOU ANYMORE UNTIL I HEAR FROM YOU JUST SO YOU KNOW I'M NOT A PSYCHO.

ELI.

SUBJECT: ARE YOU SAFE
TO: RheaVelvetKenzee@pacificlakescommunitycollege.us.net
FROM: IsaacJoesephMatthews@pacificlakescommunitycollege.us.net
RHEA,
LET ME KNOW YOU'RE OKAY.
ISAAC

SUBJECT: SORRY
TO: RheaVelvetKenzee@pacificlakescommunitycollege.us.net
FROM: EmmoryVanessaJane@pacificlakescommunitycollege.us.net

RHEA,
YOU'RE FOR REAL HUH? SORRY
TO WIG OUT ON YOU BUT YOU HAVE
TO ADMIT THAT IF YOU WEREN'T
REALLY THERE, THAT WOULD BE A
SHITTY THING TO DO. RIGHT? COME
ON GIRL…TELL ME YOU FORGIVE ME?
*EMM

SUBJECT: PO PO NOTIFIED
TO:
RheaVelvetKenzee@pacificlakescommunityc
ollege.us.net
FROM:
EmmoryVanessaJane@pacificlakescommunit
ycollege.us.net
RHEA,
I CALLED THE COLLEGE AND
ALL I GOT IN EVERY OFFICE WAS A
BUSY SIGNAL. I CALLED THE POLICE
AND I'M PRETTY SURE THEY TOOK IT
AS A PRANK. THAT, OR THEY WERE
SURPRISED THAT I KNEW ABOUT IT.
JUST WANTED YOU TO KNOW I
BELIEVE YOU.
*EMM

I took a deep breath, not really sure what I was feeling. So much for settling down with my favorite book and a good cup of coffee. I was the farthest thing from relaxed. Not only had I heard several more voices on the other side of the damn vent that I now needed to decipher, but I also had to worry about getting back to everyone before they flipped out. All I really felt like doing was pulling the covers over my head and hiding. *Ironic,* I thought…considering that's exactly what I *was* doing.

So, I pulled myself back farther from the light that seeped through the vent grates, rolled my neck and figured I'd get the most bothersome emails out of the way before I could settle in and visit with Eli. Although I was glad Emmory had called the police, she still had really pissed me off and I really didn't feel like talking to her. Isaac—wow. He was a conundrum. A message from him signed Isaac any other time would've made me giddy, but when I read it today, well…it just seemed like another fucking task I had to deal with. The only good thing was that hearing from him meant that he was probably still alive since the email came after the first three shots and the chances the last one was meant for him was rather slim in my opinion. Especially since he had said he was still safe.

I checked my battery and had never been so glad to see that it was still at 84%. One lesson I've learned is that no matter what, never leave the house without a fully charged cell phone. I stretched my fingers and began to compose…

SUBJECT: RE: ARE YOU SAFE
TO:
IsaacJoesephMatthews@pacificlakescommunitycollege.us.net
FROM:
RheaVelvetKenzee@pacificlakescommunitycollege.us.net
HI MR. MATTHEWS. YES, I AM STILL WHERE YOU PUT ME. DID YOU MAKE IT WHERE YOU WERE HEADED? THANKS FOR THINKING OF ME. I LET

MY ROOMMATE KNOW WHAT WAS
GOING ON AND SHE NOTIFIED THE
PORTLAND POLICE. I'LL KEEP YOU
POSTED.
	~RHEA~

	SUBJECT: RE: PO PO NOTIFIED
	TO:
EmmoryVanessaJane@pacificlakescommunit
ycollege.us.net
	FROM:
RheaVelvetKenzee@pacificlakescommunityc
ollege.us.net
	EMMORY,
	THANKS FOR GETTING THE
POLICE INVOLVED.
	KEEP ME POSTED.
	AS FOR US, I DON'T HAVE THE
ENERGY OR CARE RIGHT NOW TO
ADDRESS THE MESS YOU TURNED
OUR SISTERHOOD INTO. DON'T
BERATE ME WITH DRAMA FILLED
EMAILS. I'M DEALING WITH TRYIING
TO STAY ALIVE.
	~RHEA~
P.S. PRETTY MUCH FEELING LIKE
SCREW THE NEXT SEVERAL SONG
PROJECTS WE WERE WORKING ON.
YOU MADE IT PRETTY CLEAR THAT I
WAS DISPOSABLE TO YOU.

	SUBJECT: I'M FINE…SEE? <3

TO:
EliValenSnohe@pacificlakescommunitycolle
ge.us.net
FROM:
RheaVelvetKenzee@pacificlakescommunityc
ollege.us.net
ELI,
YOU'VE GOT TO STOP WITH THE
INCESSANT EMAILS—YOU'RE RIGHT,
IT'S ENOUGH TO MAKE A GIRL RUN IN
THE OPPOSITE DIRECTION, EVEN IN
AN AIR DUCT. HAHA
SORRY I MADE YOU WORRY.
THE ONLY REASON I DON'T THINK
YOU ARE CRAZY, IS IF I DIDN'T HEAR
BACK FROM YOU, I'D PROBABLY LET
MY MIND GO THERE
TOO…WORRYING I MEAN. I DOUBT
I'D SEND YOU LIKE FIVE OR SIX
EMAILS THOUGH. :-P
SO, THERE'S NEW DETAILS.
WHILE I WAS TAKING A SHORT
NAP I OBVIOUSLY MISSED THE
GUNMEN BRINGING HOSTAGES INTO
THE LAYOUT AND DESIGN
CLASSROOM. I ONLY KNOW THIS
BECAUSE I'VE HEARD FEMALE
VOICES—THEY DON'T SEEM TO BE
PART OF THE GANG.
ALSO, I GOT AHOLD OF MY
ROOMMATE AND SHE NOTIFIED THE
PORTLAND POLICE. SHE SAID SHE

CALLED SEVERAL NUMBERS AT THE
COLLEGE AND THEY WERE ALL BUSY.
        SO, YOU KNEW WHO I WAS HUH?
THAT'S COOL. I JUST WISHED I PAID
MORE ATTENTION TO WHO WAS IN
THAT CLASS. I MEAN I KNOW I'VE
SEEN YOU BUT TELL ME SOMETHING
THAT WILL MAKE YOU STAND OUT
TO ME.
        AS FAR AS HOW MY NAME WAS
CHOOSEN—WELL, MY MOM HAD ME
AND LEFT RIGHT AFTER ON
DEPLOYMENT. I ACTUALLY DIDN'T
HAVE A NAME SO MY GRAND-MIMI
NAMED ME RHEA AS IT WAS THE
MOTHER OF THE GODS. SHE THOUGHT
IT WOULD GIVE ME A FOOT-UP
SOMEHOW. YOU KNOW, HAVING
SUCH A STRONG NAME. WHICH THEN
IRONICALLY SHE CONTRASTED WITH
VELVET—SOMETHING SOFT. SO,
BASICALLY I AM YOUR ALL
AMERICAN OXIMORON. HAHA.
        WHAT ELSE? WELL, I AM FROM
ISREILI DESCENT. MY PARENTS WERE
BORN IN NY AND I WAS BORN IN CALI.
ON A NAVAL BASE. MY MOM HAD
MET MY DAD OVER SEAS IN
BAHARAIN, AND HE DIED ON A
SPECIAL OPS MISSION. IT WAS SO
COVERT THAT THERE IS ACTUALLY
NO RECORD OF IT. ALL I HAVE AS
PROOF OF MY DAD IS A FEW PICS AND

LETTERS HE SENT TO MY MOM WHEN
THEY WERE APART. I CAN TELL YOU
THIS THOUGH, WHAT THEY
HAD…WELL, IT'S EXACTLY WHAT I
WANT. IT WAS PASSIONATE, INTENSE,
AND A VERY REAL AND SUPPORTIVE
LOVE.
UGGHHH! I CANNOT BELIEVE I
AM TELLING YOU ALL OF THIS! HIT
ME UP.
~RHEA~

I hit send before I lost my courage. It took a lot from me to trust someone I barely knew with the intimate details of my past. A past that I guarded so strongly because I didn't want it tainted in any way. I loved my parents and feel cheated that I'd lost both of them to their duty for their country. *What about their duty to me?*

My attention was drawn from my reverie to the classroom. Voices were speaking in hushed and nervous bursts.

"It doesn't matter why they split us up. What matters is that they did." A scared female spoke in a worried voice. "Before they blindfolded us, did anyone see their faces or how many of them there were?"

"I'm pretty sure there were like ten of them. We were rounded up by a crew of five, then we were taken down to the first floor where there were two others and then those three who seemed to always fight came in. Did you see that big guy they called Spider? He's like a genetically modified beast."

That got a good amount of chuckles from the group. It was good to hear that they still had the ability to laugh after what they'd been through. It was also good hearing some details about Spider.

"Hey, I have an idea!" The same girl spoke and her excitement had me on the edge of my seat. "We should take details seriously and each of us should be in charge of the details of one of our captors. That way we don't have to remember everything, just the facts about our slimy gun wielding terrorist."

"That's a good idea Beth."

There was a brief pause before she responded, "Thanks Ryan."

I wondered if they had become friends out of necessity like Eli and I had, or if they were already friends before this. It wasn't long before the tone of the conversation had turned more easy-going and at times through the rest of the hour it even came off as jovial. From what I could tell, there were at least twelve people in the room, maybe as many as twenty one or two, but it was hard to make out the differences in the voices.

At times throughout the hour I had even forgotten briefly what my role was; it was almost like I was a caged animal observing everyone at the zoo. I could go so far as to say that I even felt *safe* in my cage.

Chapter
-5 Hours

My phone vibrated and the home screen flashed on. The time blared 2:14.

Hickory Dickory Dock. The mouse ran up the clock. The clock struck 2 and down it ran, Hickory Dickory Dock. Tick Tock. Tick Tock. Tick Tock...

I seriously felt like I was staring at the clock, just watching the minutes and hours flip by.

A blinking blue light.

Oh Yay! I seriously had to work on being less sarcastic. I heard the classroom door bang open and heavy boots stomped their way up the stairs to where I assumed the hostages were tied up.

Were they even tied up?

"Okay fuckers! Which one of you didn't give up your phones?" I recognized Mercy's voice, and boy was he pissed. "I gave explicit instructions on what it would take for you to stay alive!" I heard a desk fly down the stairs. "Okay, maybe you'll talk?" I heard a female whimper…then a sharp cry. "Oh. Poor baby, did that hurt? How about if I give you over to Spider to talk?"

"NO! NO! What do you want to know?" The scared girl somehow managed to squeak out a nervous response that hinged on terror.

"Crush, get over here and hold this bitch for Spider."

I heard what sounded like someone making their way through the hostages, there were grunts, 'Ows', and numerous cries like someone was purposely punishing those he came in contact with.

"Hey, Mercy—what color bra do you think this sexy mamacita is wearing?" There were crude laughs from two men, which I could easily assume came from Mercy and Crush.

"Hey, Spider-man, let's take bets? What do you say…" It sounded like the voice of reason, Crush, but then why would he do something so careless? "Well, how about we take bets from everyone and…"

"Yeah! Damn fine idea fucker. I've got it; the winners get to keep their clothes on and the *L-L-Losers* get to meet with mine and Mercy's hands?" Spider let out a sinister wolf howl while the other two men laughed.

"I'll talk, I'll talk! I told you that I'd talk. What do you want to know?"

"Fuck, Mercy—what did you ask her? Do you even give a shit? I don't know about you but I'd much rather see some tits."

God that laugh was getting so annoying. I cannot stand that guy!

"Knock it off, Spider. If she's willing to talk then get the info from her. Stay focused on the main objective. Any straying from the main plan, and shit's gonna hit the fan."

"Right, Boss." He redirected his attention to the girl. "Okay little mamacita, what's your name?" He laughed lewdly.

"E-E-Elizabeth."

"Eh. Eh. Eh…stupid fucking stutter. What are you Auh. Auh. Auh-fraid?" It sounded like that got a laugh out of Crush as well with his snide mockery.

"I swear, Spider, if you don't get the answer's I need and quit fucking around, you'll be downstairs and I'll bring Jester up here." I could hear some mumbling—*boy Spider is a real pain-in-the-ass.*

"So, Beth," it was Crush that spoke up. "Please just give Mercy the answers that he wants. He wants to know who has a phone, or a tablet, or any device that can connect with the police."

"Fuck, Crush—now they know that police were contacted. Nice job!" Spider bit out the angry riposte.

"Both of you—ENOUGH!" I heard Mercy dole out a smack to someone and a couple of hostages cried out—clearly afraid. "I'll do this myself."

I heard the hefty fall of his heavy boots on the wooden floor, stopping before someone who was whimpering.

"Hey, you don't have to be a bully—let go of her hair. She already said that she'd cooperate with you." A shrill female voice piped up.

"Spider, Crush—take her downstairs." That's all it took and she was removed. Evidently Mercy showed no mercy, and didn't take to well to any hostages showing dissention. The classroom door slammed open, banging on the wall and closed softly behind the two men who'd left with the poor girl.

"Alright love, now that we're alone, I need some details…the kind that I know you have and aren't very forthcoming with." There was a slight shuffle; I figured it came from the girl Beth.

"Sir,…"

"Call me, Mercy."

"Mercy, I can speak for everyone in this group. You put me in charge with Ryan to collect everything. We did and turned them all in to you. Really there's nothing."

"Bullshit!" He immediately got on a walkie-talkie and called Jester to come up. "Here's how this is going to go. If I don't get the truth from you guys before Jester gets up here in the next minute, then he's going to strip search you—then cavity search you. Is that understood?" The seconds tick-tocked by until the door down in front of the classroom.

"What's up, Mercy?" It was a new voice—a nasally drawl that sounded backwoods-ish.

"Strip them down. If you don't find any devices, cavity search them. I'll be back."

Mercy's heavy footsteps sounded less severe the farther from the vent he got. Then he left. The hostages were left alone with this 'hick' Mercy called Jester. My stomach tightened as I began listening to that asshole Jester have the men and women undress—completely. I couldn't listen to the sobs and cries anymore and averted my attention to my newest emails.

SUBJECT: I'M WORRIED ABOUT U AND DON'T WANT 2 FIGHT

TO: RheaVelvetKenzee@pacificlakescommunityc ollege.us.net

FROM: EmmoryVanessaJane@pacificlakescommunit ycollege.us.net

RHEA,

PLEASE LET'S NOT FIGHT. I WAS WRONG, REALLY WRONG. I CAN'T SAY SORRY ENOUGH, BUT I HATE TO EVEN THINK…WHAT IF WE'RE FIGHTING AND YOU DON'T MAKE IT. I COULDN'T LIVE WITH MYSELF. PLEASE FORGIVE ME AND LET'S CONTINUE TO CREATE BEAUTIFUL MUSIC TOGETHER.

*EMM

I sighed and opened the next in line; also from Emmory.

SUBJECT: TELL ME WHAT YOU THINK
TO: RheaVelvetKenzee@pacificlakescommunitycollege.us.net
FROM: EmmoryVanessaJane@pacificlakescommunitycollege.us.net
RHEA,
I HAVE THIS STUFF JUST KIND OF FLOATING AROUND IN MY HEAD. YOU'RE MY FAVORITE CRITIC. LMK

The morning was full of beauty. The sky a rainbow hue.
The rain had stained the pavement, but I'd just no effin' clue.
I was full of selfish joy, the narcissistic kind.
I'd punched you in the gut, but I'd just no effin' clue.
....no clue my love that you're dealing with a storm.
...no clue my love that you'd be fighting for your life.
...no clue my love that you were my bestest of friends,
until a shot rang out...rang out...staining my selfish heart.

WELL, THAT'S WHAT I HAVE SO FAR…<3

*EMM

I rolled my neck trying to ease the tension, a silent stream of tears made their way down my cheek. *I have such good friends—after all, wouldn't I have responded in a similar way if Emm had sent me a message like the one that I'd sent her? And those lyrics! She has mad talent and I'd be a fool to throw her away…like she did me.*

I sat in the tight, dark, suffocating air duct and had myself a good cry. I tried to be quiet, but I cannot say for sure that I was. I allowed myself to feel everything that had happened to me so far, and more importantly…everything that was happening to the poor souls outside my vent. I cried and silently cursed that bastard Jester and the man who had joined him not long after Mercy had left, the two of them violated the hostages with brute force and wandering hands, screams and cries assaulting my ears. I hugged my knees tightly and gently rocked myself…desperately trying to comfort myself.

Chapter
-4 Hours

It seemed like the horror on the other side of my vent had been going on forever, but when I checked my phone it only read 3:10.

Six hours? Has it really only been six fucking hours? Dear God, please help me stay strong. Lord, please help those in the other rooms stay strong. Please…

I carefully shifted my weight from one butt cheek to the other, shifting my hips ever so slightly so as not to make a single noise, trying to get the blood flow back into my legs. The men on the other side of the wall must have left the classroom seeing as how now the 'others' had gone quiet. If I strained my ears with all my might I could catch a couple of voices whispering in panicked and scared rushes. I listened for just a minute before the shear effort of trying to decipher the cryptic syllables I heard took their toll on me and the threat of a headache precariously teetered.

I rolled my neck in gentle circles trying ever so silently to get a good stretch in while I still had the chance. I bent the slightest forward before my shoulders caught on either side of the duct. I loosely and ever so slightly jounced my knees, trying just to get the lactic acid to flow out of my weary muscles. *I'm getting dehydrated, I need water.* I thought, panic rearing its ugly head again. My legs were starting to cramp up from being cooped up in such a small space.

What I wouldn't give to be outside running in the rain! Screw running and it could even be sunny and hot just so long as I made it back outside…again…someday.

I angrily swiped at a traitorous tear that snuck its way down my sweaty and dust-smeared cheek. I shrugged my shoulders trying to relieve the onslaught of tension my thoughts had caused, the terror of the last hour had caused, and focused on opening and closing my fingers into tight fists and then stretching them open until they hurt. It had been a couple of hours that I had been too afraid to take a deep breath, or make a sound let alone move. My eyes were adjusting to the lack of light coming through the filter.

They must have turned the lights off this time?

I was struggling trying to keep what was going on in my head and the terror that was happening all around me compartmentalized. I had to keep a grip on reality.

You've just got to hang on Rhea. Stay strong. You can do this.

My phone vibrated, and I decided focusing on emails would snap me from my dreary state and help me redirect my attention toward the positives.

SUBJECT: SO, HOW GOES IT?
TO:
RheaVelvetKenzee@pacificlakescommunityc
ollege.us.net
FROM:
IsaacJoesephMatthews@pacificlakescommun
itycollege.us.net
RHEA,
OKAY, I'VE BEEN
THINKING…AS ONE TENDS TO DO IN
A SITUATION WHERE ONE IS STUCK
ALONE WITH ONE'S SELF FOR SIX
HOURS AND COUNTING…
WHAT I CAME UP WITH
WAS…THAT I WOULD KICK MYSELF IF
ANYTHING WERE TO HAPPEN TO YOU

OR MYSELF WITHOUT ME TELLING YOU HOW IT IS.

SO, HERE IT GOES…

BUT, BEFORE I DO…YOU ARE GETTING AN 'A' IN THIS CLASS FOR NO OTHER REASON THAN THE TREMENDOUS EFFORT THAT YOU PUT INTO YOUR PROJECTS, THE SINCERE VOICE THAT YOU USE DURING OUR DISCUSSIONS, AND YOUR TALENT. SUFFICES TO SAY THAT YOU ARE CUT OUT FOR THE ADVERTISING WORLD.

THERE.

NOW, WHERE I WAS HEADED…

RHEA, WE HAVE BEEN CONFINED BY THE PARAMETERS OF OUR STUDENT/TEACHER RELATIONSHIP FOR THE PAST TWO…PERHAPS CLOSER TO THREE YEARS. I HAVE WATCHED YOU GROW AS A STUDENT AND A TALENTED COPYWRITER, AS I GREW MYSELF AS A PROFESSIONAL INSTRUCTOR AND PERSON. YOUR TIME IS NEARLY UP HERE AT PLCC. WHAT ARE YOUR PLANS? WHERE ARE YOU GOING FROM HERE?

I GUESS WHAT I AM TRYING TO SAY IS…

I LIKE YOU.

A LOT.

IF I DIDN'T GET THAT OUT BEFORE ONE OF US GOT HURT, I'D

NEVER FORGIVE MYSELF. SO, AT THE RISK OF LOSING MY JOB AND FELLOWSHIP…THERE IT IS.

I'LL SAY IT AGAIN…I'D SHOUT IT IF I COULD.

I REALLY LIKE YOU.

ISAAC

I sat there a little dumbfounded. *He likes me?* Hadn't I always wished that he did? Why did it take this catastrophe for him to decide that he did? Or maybe it just made telling me easier? In any case, I wasn't too sure how to respond, or what to say…hell, if he had told me even as late as yesterday—I would've been thrilled. Over the moon with excitement. Now though…well, I don't know. It just seemed…unwelcome. Another stressor in my life. Another set of feelings that relied on me to make them okay. I'd get back to him, but needed a minute to figure out how best to respond. I didn't want to hurt his feelings. So, what better way to put him off than to read what Eli had to say to me?

SUBJECT: HEY YOU!

TO: RheaVelvetKenzee@pacificlakescommunitycollege.us.net

FROM: EliValenSnohe@pacificlakescommunitycollege.us.net

SO, THAT WAS A PRETTY AWESOME LETTER! WHAT A GREAT STORY YOU HAVE TO TELL YOUR FRIENDS AND KIDS ABOUT YOUR NAME! I THINK YOUR GRANDMA MIMI

WAS A SMART LADY GIVING YOU SUCH A POWERFUL NAME. IT TOTALLY FITS YOU! <3

YOUR PARENT'S LOVE STORY…WOW! THAT IS ALL THAT I CAN SAY. WHO DOESN'T WANT THAT KIND OF LOVE? DON'T WE ALL? I THINK ESPECIALLY WHEN YOU ARE FACED WITH YOUR OWN MORTALITY…YOUR OWN EXPIRATION DATE LOOMING IN FRONT OF YOU, WELL…HOW CAN YOU NOT START THINKING ABOUT WANTING A DIFFERENT LIFE? ONE WITH MORE MEANING? A LIFE THAT IS JOINED WITH SOMEONE ELSE'S THAT WILL BRING MORE MEANING TO YOUR OWN. KNOW WHAT I MEAN?

I MIGHT BE GETTING AHEAD OF MYSELF, BUT I CANNOT IMAGINE TRYING TO FACE EACH HOUR OF THIS WITHOUT YOU HERE WITH ME. I MIGHT BE SHOOTING MYSELF IN THE FOOT (BETTER THAN OUR GUNMEN SHOOTING ME IN THE HEAD—HAHA, J/K), BUT I'M PLEASANTLY SURPRISED BY HOW EASY IT IS TO TALK TO YOU AND HOW EASILY IT HAS BEEN TO CONNECT WITH YOU ON A GENUINE AND AUTHENTIC LEVEL. YOU ARE ONE SPECIAL GIRL RHEA.

ELI.

I sat back, leaning my head quietly against the end piece of the duct. The hostages were no longer crying and had shuffled around, presumably looking for their clothing and getting dressed not long after those two assholes had left them. Now they had resorted to a calm and quiet conversation. Last I had tuned in, it was centered on motive. I had blown it off, because I'd already exhausted possible motives in my own head and was pretty over it all. Honestly, who gave a fuck what these assholes motives were? We were stuck here and as far as I knew, no help had been sent.

My mind wandered and I suddenly felt exhausted. I was so tired.

How could that be? It was only about three in the afternoon?!

First things first…

       SUBJECT: CAN I JUST SAY WOW?
       TO:
IsaacJoesephMatthews@pacificlakescommunitycollege.us.net
       FROM:
RheaVelvetKenzee@pacificlakescommunitycollege.us.net
       I'M NOT IGNORING YOU.
       AFTER READING WHAT YOU WROTE ME ALL I COULD THINK WAS WOW.
       SORRY.
       THANKS FOR YOUR HONESTY. I JUST NEED TO STEW ON IT FOR AWHILE.
       ~RHEA~

I hit send with a heavy heart. I knew he had wanted a different response, but it was all that I could give him. Emmory's and Eli's emails were going to be so much easier to respond to…

SUBJECT: DITTO <3
TO: EliValenSnohe@pacificlakescommunitycollege.us.net
FROM: RheaVelvetKenzee@pacificlakescommunitycollege.us.net
ELI,
FIRST OF ALL, YOU DON'T NEED TO WORRY ABOUT SOUNDING A CERTAIN WAY. CLEARLY OR NOT QUITE SO CLEARLY; I FEEL THE SAME WAY. IT'S FUNNY TO SAY, AND IT IS BEYOND MY UNDERSTANDING, BUT I AM SURE THAT I FEEL THE SAME WAY THAT YOU DO. THE THING IS, IF I STOP TO WONDER WHY…I CAN'T EXPLAIN IT.
I MEAN, WHY DO YOU SUPPOSE WE LIKE EACH OTHER SO MUCH? IS IT BECAUSE WE HAVE A GENUINE CONNECTION? PERHAPS…
IS IT BECAUSE WE FEEL ALONE AND ISOLATED?
ABSOLUTELY…
IS IT BECAUSE THERE ISN'T AND WILL NEVER BE ANOTHER PERSON WHO WILL COMPRHEND

WHAT IT MEANS TO BE CONSUMED WITH FEAR FOR YOUR LIFE WHILE HIDING FROM DERRANGED GUNMEN? ABSOUTELY.

SO, I MEAN I CARE A LOT FOR YOU. I WORRY ABOUT YOU. I WANT TO KNOW EVERYTHING THERE IS ABOUT YOU AND INSTEAD OF BEING MY TYPICAL ANALYTICAL SELF…I HAVE DECIDED TO JUST FEEL FOR A CHANGE.

SO, I FEEL LIKE I WANT MORE OF YOU ELI. MORE AND MORE AND MORE.

~RHEA~

I sat there in the near complete darkness after I hit send and my phone screen went dark. My ears were hot and I had a tangible lump in my throat. If I'd had a mirror I am quite certain that I'd be blushing. It was almost comical how worked up I had gotten baring my soul to Eli…suppressing a nervous laugh was pretty darn hard at this point. I opened my email to Emmory just as the classroom door banged open and the lights were thrown back on.

"Alright fuckers! On your feet!"

I tried my damnedest to identify who the voice came from but couldn't place it. It wasn't Mercy, Crush, or the low menacing voice that Spider had. Jester maybe? One of the others? It was too soon to tell.

"So, the police are outside and demanding that we show them that everyone is alive before our demands are met. Who thinks they've been good enough to go on a fieldtrip?"

"Before we do anything, could we have a bathroom break?" It sounded like the man Ryan—who had asked.

"Yes, please? We really need to go." Beth the girl from before chimed in. It was easy to tell hers and Ryan's voice from the others. He sounded like he had a sore throat and hers was that teeny tiny little girls voice that you hear every great once in a while.

The captor grumbled and apparently agreed because they all filed out the door as it gently closed behind them.

I'm alone. Completely and utterly alone.

The thought that at times in my past would've scared me or caused a fair amount of panic, now only brought me peace. I was beyond glad that I was ALL ALONE. I tossed my purse down the duct pass the vent opening and slid my butt down the length of the duct until I had space to lay down. Just a little nap, a little nap was all I needed. I was just so damn tired.

Chapter
0.0 Hours

I was startled awake. I glanced at my phone—7:15. I listened, every hair on my body was on edge. I had no idea what had caused me to wake up three hours in to my nap, but something wasn't right. As far as I could tell, nobody was in the classroom. I heard very faint and muffled screams, panic.

A SHOT RANG.

My heart accelerated as it was followed by a second and then by an immediate third.

Three more shots. Oh My God! Maybe I was awakened by a shot...that would be four! What in the hell is going on?

As much as I had needed my rest, I now felt like I was in the dark...so to speak. I had no frame of reference as to why there was shooting all of a sudden and what had been the precursor to those shots being fired. All I knew was that the classroom was quiet. DEADLY QUIET.

I dragged my purse over to where I was laying and pulled myself up into a seated position back in the dead-end duct. My phone was blinking so I swiped the screen—seven emails were staring back at me. The first was the email Emmory had sent me earlier and there was one more from her, two from Isaac and three from Eli. Bending my head to look down at my phone made me realize just how sore I had become, what I wouldn't give to stand. Hell, what I wouldn't give to be out of this fucked up mess.

Shit, like I even know how to go about it?

SUBJECT: THINKING ABOUT YOU

TO:
RheaVelvetKenzee@pacificlakescommunityc
ollege.us.net
FROM:
EmmoryVanessaJane@pacificlakescommunit
ycollege.us.net
RHEA,
I OBVIOUSLY COULDN'T THINK,
OR FOCUS ON SINGING TODAY, SO
I'VE LEFT THE STUDIO. I'M NOT
TELLING YOU THIS FOR ANY REASON
OTHER THAN TO LET YOU KNOW HOW
IMPORTANT YOU ARE TO ME. I JUST
DON'T EVEN KNOW WHAT I WOULD
DO WITHOUT YOU.
PLEASE DON'T BE MAD THAT I
AM SHARING, IT'S NOT TO MAKE YOU
FEEL BADLY THAT I ENDED THE
RECORDING BEFORE FINISHING—
LUCKILY THE GUYS HERE WERE VERY
UNDERSTANDING AND THEY'RE
LETTING ME RESCHEDULE AFTER
EVERYTHING AT THE COLLEGE ENDS.
I MISS YOU RHE-RHE. JUST
KNOW I LOVE YOU, HAVE YOU IN MY
THOUGHTS CONSTANTLY, AND AM
PRAYING FOR YOUR SAFETY.
*EMM

SUBJECT: UPDATE
TO:
RheaVelvetKenzee@pacificlakescommunityc
ollege.us.net

FROM: <u>EmmoryVanessaJane@pacificlakescommunitycollege.us.net</u>

RHEA,

SO, HERE'S THE UPDATE.

I CALLED THE POLICE AND THOSE ASSHOLES WERE ABSOLUTELY NO HELP AT ALL AS FAR AS TELLING ME WHAT WAS GOING ON WITH THE SITUATION.

SO, I GOT MY MOM INVOLVED UP AT THE GOVENOR'S OFFICE. THEY HAD NO IDEA THAT PLCC WAS UNDER ATTACK OR THAT THERE WAS AN ACTIVE HOSTAGE SITUATION.

I UPDATED HER ON THE FIRES SHOT SO FAR AND POSSIBLE DEATH COUNT.

I KNOW THAT THE GOVENOR HAS MADE A CALL TO THE

LOCAL POLICE, BUT THE REPORT THAT SHE'S GOTTEN IS THAT THE LOCAL POLICE HAVE BEEN IN CONTACT WITH THE PERPETRATORS AND SINCE THEY DON'T NEGOTIATE WITH 'TERRORISTS', THEY'RE PLAYING A WAITING GAME. AT THIS POINT IT SEEMS NEITHER SIDE IS WILLING TO BUDGE.

ALL CRAP IF YOU ASK ME. IT SEEMS THEY'D BE TRYING TO GET YOU OUT OF THERE AS QUICKLY AS POSSIBLE.

STAY STRONG. IT WILL ALL
WORK OUT; IT ALWAYS SEEMS TO
WHEN YOU ARE CONCERNED.
LUCKY BITCH! <3
*EMM

*Lucky bitch? Is she fucking serious? OH YEAH, I am
so lucky cooped up in a fucking air duct!*

I leaned back against the duct-end and sighed heavily.
I couldn't say that I was tired exactly—I'd just had about as
peaceful a nap as one could under these conditions; however,
I just couldn't shake the fatigue that I felt. I was exhausted
from the emotional rollercoaster that I was on. The last email
took me for another loop-de-loop. I had gotten so hopeful for
those couple of seconds before I'd reached the end of the
email when the wind had been ripped from my sails. It
sucked because all I wanted to do was have a little hope. A
little optimism that all of this was on its way to a happy
ending. An ending that marked my never having to sit alone
in a dark, lonely, confined space ever again.

SUBJECT: RE: UPDATE
TO:
EmmoryVanessaJane@pacificlakescommunit
ycollege.us.net
FROM:
RheaVelvetKenzee@pacificlakescommunityc
ollege.us.net
EMM,
THANKS FOR THE UPDATE. I
APPRECIATE YOUR MOM GETTING
INVOLVED—SEE HER WORKING FOR
THE GOVENOR PAYS OFF.

REMEMBER IN HIGH SCHOOL HOW WE HATED HER POSITION AND HOW IT CRAMPED OUR STYLE? WELL, I HAVE TO GRUDINGY ADMIT I DON'T MIND SO MUCH NOW. HEHE

SO A FEW UPDATES ON MY END. THERE'S BEEN I THINK LIKE FOUR MORE GUN SHOTS. I TOOK A NAP AND AM NOT SURE WHAT HAPPENED WHILE I WAS OUT, BUT THE HOSTAGES ARE NO LONGER IN THE COPY AND LAYOUT CLASSROOM ON THE SECOND FLOOR…SO, PRESUMABLY THEY WERE MOVED DOWNSTAIRS, BUT I DON'T KNOW FOR SURE.

I SHOULD ALSO MENTION THAT THE HOSTAGES WERE STRIP SEARCHED AND CAVITY SEARCHED…AND FROM THE SOUNDS OF IT VIOLATED IN FIFTY DIFFERENT WAYS. I AM SURE MEDICS ARE NEEDED.

I HAVE A COUPLE OF EMAILS FROM MY INSTRUCTOR ISAAC MATTHEWS—ALTHOUGH I AM PUTTING OFF READING THEM BECAUSE HE TOLD ME HE LIKED ME IN THE LAST EMAIL. I'M PROCRASTINATING READING THEM— YOU KNOW ME CAUSE I JUST DON'T WANT TO DEAL WITH THE STRESS OF HAVING ANOTHER PERSON'S

FEELINGS REVOLVE AROUND ME.
BASICALLY HE SAID THAT IF HE
NEVER HAD THE CHANCE TO TELL ME,
HE'D REGRET IT. SO, HE DID.
        UPDATE, UPDATE, UPDATE…
WELL, THERE IS ONE MORE THNG.
I'VE MET SOMEONE. HAHA…ONLY ME
RIGHT? AND AS A SIDE I WAS PISSED
WHEN I READ YOU THOUGHT I WAS A
LUCKY BITCH…BUT WHO ELSE
WOULD HAVE THE LUCK TO MEET
SOMEONE THEY GENUINELY LIKE
FROM AN AIR DUCT?
        HOW FUNNY IT TOOK TELLING
YOU ABOUT ELI TO REALIZE THAT
HE'S PRETTY SPECIAL AND THAT I DO
HAVE SOMETHING GOING FOR ME.
        SO, INSTEAD OF RIPPING YOU
AN NEW ASSHOLE HERE AT THE END,
I GUESS I'LL JUST END BY SAYING…
        THANK YOU AND I LOVE YOU.
        ~RHEA~

I sat back and smiled. Eli. I really wanted to read his emails next, but decided instead to get the chore of Isaac's out of the way.

        SUBJECT: YOUR STEW
        TO:
RheaVelvetKenzee@pacificlakescommunityc
ollege.us.net

FROM: IsaacJoesephMatthews@pacificlakescommunitycollege.us.net

RHEA,

OKAY, I'M DYING TO KNOW HOW THAT 'STEW' IS TURNING OUT. HAHA

NO, BUT SERIOUSLY. I TOTALLY UNDERSTAND WHAT A SHOCK IT MIGHT BE FOR YOU SEEING AS HOW WE HAVE ALWAYS HAD NOTHING BUT THE 'DEFINITION' OF A PROFESSOR/STUDENT RELATIONSHIP. OF COURSE I COULDN'T LET ON THAT I ADMIRED YOU SO, AND I'M HOPING THAT IF WE COME OUT OF THIS 'OKAY'—WHATEVER THAT ENDS UP BEING—THAT IF YOU DON'T RECIPROCATE MY FEELINGS, THAT THEY STAY BETWEEN YOU AND I. OF COURSE I AM SURE THAT GOES WITHOUT SAYING, AS COOL AS YOU ARE.

…JUST THINKING, SEEING AS I HAVE NOTHING BUT TIME ON MY HANDS.

ISAAC

SUBJECT: DINNER
TO: RheaVelvetKenzee@pacificlakescommunitycollege.us.net

FROM:
IsaacJoesephMatthews@pacificlakescommun
itycollege.us.net
RHEA,
NO MATTER HOW THIS ENDS.
NO MATTER WHAT YOU THINK
OR FEEL.
NO MATTER…
WHEN THIS IS ALL OVER I AM
TAKING YOU OUT FOR THE BEST THAI
FOOD IN TOWN.
ISAAC.

I subconsciously found myself trying to roll my neck
to remove the tightness in my muscles that had noticeably
tightened while I'd read Isaac's emails. Maybe I shouldn't
be so singular in my choices. It's not like there wasn't time
to get to know both; so why was I letting Isaac work me up
into a stressed out tizzy and in contrast, falling for Eli?
Especially after such a short time. It was weird, but then
what about all this craziness wasn't a little?

SUBJECT: TAG YOU'RE IT!
TO:
IsaacJoesephMatthews@pacificlakescommun
itycollege.us.net
FROM:
RheaVelvetKenzee@pacificlakescommunityc
ollege.us.net
ISAAC,
WELL, I HAVE STIRRED AND
STIRRED THE STEW SO-TO-SPEAK AND

WHAT I'VE COME UP WITH WILL
PROBABLY SURPRISE YOU.
      SO, YES. I WAS CONSIDERABLY
TAKEN OFF GUARD. I DON'T REALLY
KNOW WHAT THE HELL MY PROBLEM
WAS, CAUSE—AND NOW IT'S MY
TURN TO BE HONEST—I HAVE LIKED
YOU QUITE A BIT SINCE MY
COPYWRITING BASICS CLASS THAT I
HAD WITH YOU FALL SEMESTER OF
MY SOPHOMORE YEAR.
      SURPRISED? THERE'S MORE…

I took a deep breath trying to find the courage to
continue—after all, what did I have to lose—and as Isaac
had pointed out; there was a distinct possibility that we
might not make it out of here. So what was the harm in
being truly honest?

      NOT ONLY DID I LIKE YOU, BUT
YOU CAN ASK PRETTY MUCH
ANYONE IN THE JOURNALISM
SCHOOL, AND THOSE THAT HAVE
KNOWN ME KNOW THAT I HAVE
JOKINGLY ACKNOWLEDGED MY
UNDYING LOVE FOR YOU…
      HAHA. JUST KIDDING.
      NO, BUT REALLY. I'VE SHARED
THAT I LIKE YOU TOO.
      I THINK THAT INSTEAD OF
BEING OVER THE TOP ELATED THAT
YOU RECIPROCATED FEELINGS THAT
HAVE BEEN GROWING FOR YOU, IT

CAME AT A TIME WHEN I'D CLOSED
OFF MY HEART TO THAT POSSIBILITY
AND IT HAD BEEN FILLED BY
SOMEONE ELSE.
YUP. YOU HEARD ME RIGHT.

A loud bang in the dark classroom startled the crap out of me and I turned my phone off. The air duct went dark. I heard footsteps climbing the stairs, getting louder as the heavy feet landed, creaking on each of the old wooden stairs.

I dared not breathe.

I dared not move.

Every hair on my body was standing. Each beat of my heart brought the deafening sound of pulsating blood to my ears.

Was my phone off? God I hope vibrate isn't on!

The heavy boots stopped at the top of the stairs.

"Alright little mamacita," the threatening voice belonging to Spider spoke. "I know Mercy doesn't think you are here. But I have a feeling—a sixth sense that is *NEVER*, EVER wrong." A cruel snicker snaked out of his mouth. I heard him crouch down in front of the vent. He was so close I could hear him breathing and smell the stench of stale tobacco in the air. "Are you in there chica?"

I closed my eyes tightly and tried to focus on breathing as shallowly as possible, afraid he could hear the air seeping over my lips in hushed, panicked breaths. I pushed my drawn knees even tighter together, afraid he could hear them knocking.

"Ahhh, YES! You *are* in there. I knew it." I heard him stand and thought for sure he was going to leave. Instead, he bent over, and hissed into the vent. "I'm coming for you…"

His heavily receding footsteps should've been a welcoming sound, but I was too afraid to even draw in a calming breath.

What am I going to do? Jesus. How does he know? What am I going to do?

It took me a couple of minutes after I heard the heavy classroom door slam, to finally get a grip on my nerves and calm the response my body had had from the adrenaline assault it had just gone through. I allowed myself to take in a deep cleansing breath and pushed it out forcefully as though I were expelling all the bad juju with it.

I'm not for sure how long I sat there alone in the dark, too afraid to even swipe my cell screen and get back to my emails. I just couldn't shake the feeling that Spider wasn't gone.

I'm so going to need therapy after this.

I chuckled silently to myself, then grabbed for my phone and swiped it. The bright light of the home screen illuminated the dark duct and I prayed no one from out THERE could see it through the vent. I skimmed what I had typed Isaac about how I liked him but didn't immediately reciprocate his feelings and reread the last paragraph…

I THINK THAT INSTEAD OF BEING OVER THE TOP ELATED THAT YOU RECIPROCATED FEELINGS THAT I'VE BEEN GROWING FOR YOU, IT CAME AT A TIME WHEN I'D CLOSED OFF MY HEART TO THAT POSSIBILITY AND IT HAD BEEN FILLED BY SOMEONE ELSE. YUP. YOU HEARD ME RIGHT.

I'VE MET SOMEONE ELSE
THROUGH EMAIL ON THE SCHOOL'S
EMAIL INTERFACE. THAT DOESN'T
MEAN THAT I DON'T WANT TO DO
DINNER. I AM OPEN TO POSSIBILTIES
OF US.
~RHEA~

As immediately as I hit send, my phone vibrated and I saw that Isaac had already emailed me back. There was no way that he could've read my note, so I was curious to see what he had to say.

SUBJECT: **MOVE!!**
TO:
RheaVelvetKenzee@pacificlakescommunityc ollege.us.net
FROM:
IsaacJoesephMatthews@pacificlakescommun itycollege.us.net
GET THE FUCK OUT OF THERE NOW. THEY'RE COMING FOR YOU.
ISAAC.

My breath hitched again in my throat. Then my body sprang into action. I jammed my phone into my purse and quickly navigated the air duct space until I was on all fours. I had hung my purse around my neck and as I began to crawl down the tight duct, I pulled it along beneath me. I no longer worried that I'd be heard; they already knew I was there.
How did Isaac know?
The air duct was dark since little to no light now came through the vents that led to the other

classrooms…now that it was sometime between seven and eight in the evening. I paused just long enough for it to register that I had been in this duct for somewhere close to ten hours now. My stomach growled hungrily in protest to my moving forward. I navigated the duct work turning right, then left, another right and left…trying to put as much space between me and the monsters as I could.

STOP!

My brain screamed for my arms and legs to quit their blind search in the dark. I had heard the loud noise, but it hadn't consciously registered. Thank God some part of me could still decode the sounds and signs that my body was receiving. I hunched on all fours—sore as I had been seeking for a new place to hide for a good ten or fifteen minutes, as best a guess as I could make.

My wrists ached from the angle I had had them bent at, and my knees burned from crawling over all the tall rivets I had crept over. In my silence, I heard banging echoing through the duct work and loud voices arguing.

"Goddamn it, shine it in there." I could hear a muffled retort. "Fuck! Right there. Shine it there. I swear, I saw a reflection earlier." That voice was easily recognizable—it was that mean bastard Spider.

There was more arguing and I heard the vent cover bang loudly on the classroom floor.

"I can't. Why don't you try? You're damn near smaller than me…I don't give a shit, take a look!" I heard more banging and some disgruntled grunts made their way to my ears. Best as I could guess, someone was trying to squeeze into the duct space that I had called my safe haven for the past several hours.

Thank God Isaac had emailed me and that I just happened to open it immediately. Thank you God. Thank you.

I finished my silent prayer and found a surprising smile on my face at the thought of Isaac. I shrugged it off and continued silently. A few tight turns later and I found myself at a pitch black dead-end where the only duct work available for me to navigate took me up. I shined my cell phone flashlight app. up the duct and rotating my hips, sat against the dead-end. There was no way that I could make it up the wall to the next floor. At least nobody could find me through all the duct work I had crawled through—that brought me some comfort.

My stomach growled again and after searching every zipper and pocket in my purse, I gave up. I had no food. No snack. Not even gum…I was screwed. I wrapped my fingers around my phone and swiped the screen as I pulled it from my purse.

Chapter
+1 Hours

My screen read 830 pm. Another distracting stomach growl made it hard to focus on my emails, but there was absolutely no light where I was and only the faintest light coming from the 'T' that I had turned in from, a good twenty-five feet or so away from me. I knew it was only a matter of time before I'd have to leave as find a bathroom, I could feel the uncomfortable pressure already.

SUBJECT: HOW DID YOU KNOW?
TO:
IsaacJoesephMatthews@pacificlakescommun itycollege.us.net
FROM:
RheaVelvetKenzee@pacificlakescommunityc ollege.us.net
ISAAC,
HOW DID YOU KNOW? I AM SAFE FOR NOW BUT I HAVE NO IDEA WHERE I AM. I WAS TOO PANICKED TO PAY ATTENTION TO THE LEFTS AND RIGHTS THAT I TOOK, BUT I AM NOW IN A PITCH BLACK DEAD-END WITH NO WAY TO GO BUT UP OR BACK THE WAY I CAME.
TALK TO ME. I'M SCARED. THEY TRIED TO COME IN TO GET ME.
~RHEA~

The muscles in my back spasmed and my neck replied with an aggravating twitch. I wasn't too sure how much longer I could stay in this air duct before my muscles completely locked up on me. That, and my bladder was complaining—I'd have to find a bathroom before it started screaming at me. I rolled my neck and tried to get comfortable, I was finally going to read Eli's emails and I smiled at just the thought.

SUBJECT: MORE OF ME EHH? ;-)
TO: RheaVelvetKenzee@pacificlakescommunitycollege.us.net
FROM: EliValenSnohe@pacificlakescommunitycollege.us.net
SO, AT THE RISK OF SOUNDING REPETITIVE…THAT WAS A PRETTY AWESOME LETTER!
ALL I CAN THINK RIGHT NOW IS THAT YOU WANT MORE OF ME…HEHE.
DON'T WORRY, I'LL PULL MY MIND OUT OF THE GUTTER. I CAN BEHAVE AND I SUPPOSE THERE'S NO BETTER TIME TO SHOW YOU THAN WHEN I HAVE YOU AS A CAPTIVE AUDIENCE.
SO, I WAS THINKING…WHAT DO WE DO ONCE WE GET OUT OF HERE? DO WE GO ON A FIRST DATE OR DO WE COUNT THIS AS ONE? LET ME KNOW YOUR THOUGHTS.
ELI.
P.S. I'M LEANING TOWARD COUNTING THIS AS LIKE OUR FIRST FIVE DATES, CAUSE WHEN I SEE YOU STANDING

THERE OKAY BEFORE ME…WELL, IT'S
GOING TO BE PRETTY DAMN HARD
NOT TO GRAB YOU, PULL YOU TO ME
AND KISS YOU WITH EVERY, SINGLE,
FIBER OF MY BEING. AND I JUST
DON'T DO THAT ON A FIRST
DATE…JUST SAYIN'.

I was grinning ear to ear as I clicked on his next email, hoping there was some more good stuff in there. He'd made me blush at his interpretation of what I meant when I had said I had wanted more and more of him and my heart sped up as I read about the kiss he wanted to give me.

SUBJECT: EYE CANDY
TO:
RheaVelvetKenzee@pacificlakescommunityc
ollege.us.net
FROM:
EliValenSnohe@pacificlakescommunitycolle
ge.us.net
SO, IN YOUR SILENCE I CAME
TO THE REALIZATION THAT I COULD
JUST SEND YOU A PHOTO OF ME. SO…
BOOM!
HERE YA GO BABY!!
ELI.

I clicked on the attachment and my screen was filled with a familiar face. Where Isaac was a more conservative and contemporary-sexy blend of Bradley Cooper meets Paul Walker, meets sexy college professor; Eli was a rougher, rebellious melding of Adam Levine's tattoos, meets John

Depp's hair, and Ian Somerhalder's build and attitude in the Vampire Diaries. Either way I chose, I had died and gone to heaven. I didn't even bother to pull up the last email from him, all I wanted to do was put down my reaction so that what I wrote was as real and authentic as possible.

SUBJECT: RE: EYE CANDY
TO:
EliValenSnohe@pacificlakescommunitycollege.us.net
FROM:
RheaVelvetKenzee@pacificlakescommunitycollege.us.net
OH MY GOD.
BOOM IS RIGHT!
WHY DIDN'T YOU TELL ME WHO YOU WERE? YOU KNEW DAMNED WELL I HAD NOTICED YOU…JUST TELL ME EXACTLY WHO HASN'T?
~RHEA~

I skimmed my finger across the email icon and opened the last email from Eli just as my blue notification light started blinking.

Yay! Another email!

SUBJECT: WORRIED
TO:
RheaVelvetKenzee@pacificlakescommunitycollege.us.net

FROM:
EliValenSnohe@pacificlakescommunitycolle
ge.us.net

I'M SURE YOU'VE HEARD THE
MOST RECENT SHOTS.

WHAT DOES THAT PUT THE
COUNT AT…EIGHT?

BEST AS I CAN TELL THE VOICE
OF REASON, THE ONE GUY THAT
WOULD COME CLOSE TO WHERE I
WAS AND WHO SEEMED LIKE HE HAD
A MORAL HEAD ON HIS
SHOULDERS…WELL, I'M PRETTY
SURE HE WAS SHOT IN A SCUFFLE.

AFTER THEY LEFT I CHECKED
OUT THE ROOM AND THERE WAS A
LOT OF BLOOD.

A LOT.

I'M OKAY, JUST WORRIED
ABOUT YOU. THEY'RE EITHER
TALKING ABOUT YOU OR ANOTHER
PERSON HIDING IN THE WALLS. STAY
SAFE AND BE CAREFUL.

ELI.

My fingers flew across the touch screen keyboard on
my phone, they couldn't move fast enough…

SUBJECT: RE: WORRIED
TO:
EliValenSnohe@pacificlakescommunitycolle
ge.us.net

FROM:
RheaVelvetKenzee@pacificlakescommunityc
ollege.us.net
THANKS FOR THE WARNING,
I'LL TAKE HEED.
THOUGHT IT WAS ONLY RIGHT
FOR ME TO ISSUE YOU A WARNING AS
WELL…
WHEN WE GET OUT OF HERE,
YOUR FRIENDS MAY PUT OUT AN APB
ON YOUR ASS…SEEING AS HOW I
PLAN TO KIDNAP YOU AND MAKE
YOU BEG FOR THAT KISS YOU
WANTED. ☺
~RHEA~

I couldn't stop smiling, even after hearing that the gunmen were on the lookout for me. My fingers clicked on my new email icon.

SUBJECT: CHECKING UP
TO:
RheaVelvetKenzee@pacificlakescommunityc
ollege.us.net
FROM:
EsiahJosephCurn@pacificlakescommunitycol
lege.us.net
RHE,
EMM CALLED ME AND TOLD ME
WHAT IS GOING ON THERE AT THE
COLLEGE. SHE SAID IT'S BEEN
AWHILE SINCE SHE CHECKED IN WITH

YOU, BUT THAT AS FAR AS SHE KNEW…YOU WERE OKAY.

THAT WASN'T GOOD ENOUGH FOR ME.

SO, I'M WRITING YOU EVEN THOUGH I HAVE NO BUSINESS TO AFTER HOW I ENDED THINGS.

KRIS AND I ARE OVER, ALTHOUGH I AM GUESSING YOU DON'T GIVE A SHIT AND PROBABLY WISH WE WEREN'T. THEN AT LEAST YOU'D KNOW I RECEIVE A DAILY DOSE OF TORTURE. I SHOULDN'T HAVE CHEATED ON YOU. I SHOULDN'T HAVE LIED. I SHOULD'VE SAID SORRY LONG BEFORE NOW INSTEAD OF ACTING LIKE A RIGHTEOUS ASSHOLE.

SO…

I AM SORRY.

I AM VERY SORRY.

NO.

IT'S MORE THAN THAT. I HAVE A DEEP REGRET ABOUT HOW I TREATED YOU AND A STABBING GUILT THAT I CANNOT SHAKE ABOUT WHAT I DID TO YOU. I AM SO, VERY SORRY.

I KNOW THAT ISN'T ENOUGH, AND I AGREE. IT DOESN'T QUITE TOUCH ON THE FEELINGS THAT I FEEL.

I DON'T MEAN TO HIT YOU WITH ALL OF THIS WHILE YOU ARE IN

THERE, BUT IF I DIDN'T TAKE THIS CHANCE AND SOMETHING WERE TO HAPPEN TO YOU…FUCK, I JUST DON'T KNOW WHAT I'D DO.

I GUESS I JUST NEED TO KNOW THAT YOU ARE OKAY. I NEED TO KNOW THAT YOU FORGIVE ME AND HAVE MOVED PAST WHAT WE HAD.

…EVEN IF I HAVEN'T.

I'LL TELL YOU RHE—REGRET IS A BITCH AND THERE'S NO AMOUNT OF PUSSY THAT WILL OR HAS CURED ME OF YOU.

FOR ALL IT'S WORTH.

SORRY.

LOVE,

ESIAH

I sat my phone down, drawing my knees up to my chest. I swiped at the stray tears that made their way down my cheeks, then threw my hands around my knees. I lay my head on my knees…

How was I supposed to know that Esiah still loved me?

I couldn't shake the feeling that if I had only stuck around, if I had not dropped Kris's friendship like a bad habit…that Esiah and I would still be together; that was what I had wanted all these past months wasn't it? I hadn't noticed that more renegade tears had escaped from my eyes and I angrily brushed them away. Problem was, they weren't stopping.

"Are you there?"

Oh my God—I'm going crazy. I'm hearing voices!

"Hey, are you there?"

My heart slammed into my chest. Someone was whispering through an air vent. I had to be quiet. Very, *very* quiet. My body reacted immediately, pulling itself into an even tighter ball as I slinked even deeper into the inky blackness. I was pretty good at becoming invisible.

"Are you there? Rhea, answer me if you are."

SILENCE. I had to be completely silent. I WAS NOT HERE. Nobody, especially not THEM, could know I was in the walls.

"Rhea Kenzee? Rhea!" A deafening silence followed.

How do they know my name? Surely someone held hostage must have told them I stayed back to talk to Isaac. Surely someone ratted us out. Why would anyone want to hurt Mr. Matthews or me?

I heard a shuffle or rattle of some sort coming from the air duct above my head. Then again, I heard a familiar voice—but not from Mercy or Spider, and not from any other gunman that I'd heard today.

"Goddamn it Rhea, if you're there, answer me!"

"Who, who is it," I managed to squeak out through my fear and past my dry, cracked lips.

"It's Isaac."

My lungs forcefully exhaled the air I had trapped inside them while I had been holding my breath.

"Isaac," my voice waivered from sheer disbelief. "Where are you? How did you know…I mean, how did you find me?" My questions came in quick hurried whispers. I was still terrified that the gunmen would find me.

"Just a minute, someone's coming."

I heard him scrambling and then a door from the room above me bang against the wall as it was tossed open. I could just vaguely make out voices, but they diminished as they left the classroom. I heard more movement above me through the vent and what sounded like the door clicking shut.

"Rhea, are you still there?"

I breathed a sigh of relief. "Yes Isaac. I am so glad to hear your voice. I've been so worried about you…there were those gun shots, and, and…" my voice cracked and trailed off cluing him into the fears that I'd had.

"I've been looking for you."

"How did you find me?"

"I went to the vent I put you in, and you were gone. I was so incredibly worried." Now it was his turn, as his voice cracked from emotion—cluing me into the fact that he'd really meant what he said when he said he'd cared for me as more than just a student. "I've been sneaking from room to room since I got your email that you were nearly caught." I heard him pause for a deep breath, "Damn it Rhea, you just can't even imagine the thoughts that have been running through my head."

I caught myself nodding as though he could see me. "You know, I probably have a pretty good idea." A nervous laugh bubbled out of me.

"Yeah, I guess you probably do."

"Hey Isaac?"

"Yes?"

"When are we getting out of here? How can I get out of here—ya know I am pretty stuck."

"I'm not for sure, as far as timeframe goes. I've heard that the gunmen hijacked the college's computer network and had planned to confiscate passwords, account numbers, all the financial information that would allow them access to tens of millions of dollars."

I guess my gasp was louder than I had intended.

"I know right?" His voice echoed my own disbelief. "Evidently, their plan as best as the detectives can say right now…was to lock down the School of Journalism and throw the rest of the college into a tizzy trying to figure out why none of the computer systems worked. In their own deranged brilliance they'd thought that they'd have the financials confiscated, and the hostages released before anyone was the wiser."

"I don't know. It just doesn't sound like a plan that would work to me." My dubious tone wasn't hard to miss. "So, then what happened? Why did it turn into all of this? Why are people dead and for God's sake, why aren't we free yet?"

"I wish I was down there with you." His pained voice tugged on my heart strings.

"Me too Isaac. Me too."

"So Rhea, what they didn't plan on was you."

"Me? What did I do?"

"Well, somehow you got in touch with some other students here at the 'J' School via email. You see, it seems they'd shut down the campus internet so they thought nobody could communicate with the outside. You, however…you emailed your roommate, and although she had a college email, she wasn't here on campus. You blew the whole thing wide open."

"Me? It was Eli that got in touch with me."

"Eli?"

"Yes. Eli Snohe is in some of my other advertising and copywriting classes. He's the one that sent *me* an email. I just responded to him."

"Well, for whatever reason—you were the only one who got the news of what had happened off campus. I mean, without the details that you've sent your roommate—what's her name?"

"Emmory."

"Right, well without you sending Emmory all the details, she couldn't have gone to the police. I mean from what I've read in emails—they're counting the minutes until the emails you send Emmory come through. They can't wait to get the details."

"I don't get it. If I can send out emails to other people here at the school…why can't you or anyone else?"

"Well, Rhea, it's not that we can't. It's just that we didn't think to try." He paused for a second before continuing. "Like I said before, I really appreciate your 'out-of-the-box' thinking. In fact, it's one of the main reasons that I find you so intriguing in class—it's awesome to know that it's just how you are. Who you are."

I felt a blush creeping up my neck before it pooled in my cheeks.

"Rhea?"

"Yeah?"

"Earlier today you had said that you had closed off your heart and the space that you'd been saving for someone was now filled."

"Isaac, everything is so complicated right now…hell, I mean; here I am sitting in a damn air duct whispering to you. Everything hangs in the balance and it all depends on whether we make it out of here alive. Ya know?"

"I hear what you're saying but I guess I just look at it differently than you."

"Oh? How so?"

"Well…you seem like your every next movements are taken with trepidation; that all of your pent-up anxiety and nervousness is keeping you from seizing the day."

"Oh yeah—Carpe Diem right?" I softly chuckled.

"It's really no laughing matter. Rhea, you are so paralyzed by fear and by our situation that you can't find the optimism needed to take a step forward towards your future."

"You mean, like with you?" I rolled my neck from side to side, the tension Isaac's line of questioning was generating made this whole exchange a little tedious for me. But, I had to give it to him, he was right on all counts. I *didn't* want to commit to anything right now—what was the point?

"Well, yes—like with me." His concession fell hard into the deep silence that was filling the space between us. I heard him clear his throat, "Rhea?"

"Yeah, Isaac?"

"You mentioned Eli emailed you, and earlier you had said that you had met someone through the school's email system…the person that you've met. The one who filled the vacancy in your heart—was it him?"

I shrugged, although a lot of good it did me—it's not like he could see me through the wall and a floor down. "I said I wasn't closed off to a dinner with you. Getting to know you over Thai sounded like a great plan." I sighed more heavily than I had meant to.

"Rhea, I'm not trying to make you uncomfortable. I just didn't want to miss this opportunity of getting to know you and telling you how I felt. I know that there will never be another person, hell another *girl* like you that could comprehend the life-altering experience that we're going through." He paused as though searching for the right words, "I just didn't want any regrets is all…and it seems like lately all I've had are regrets." I heard a soft thud against the vent as though he had rest his head against it.

"Isaac—hell, I don't even know how or where to start but I can try to talk it through with you…that is, if you're willing to listen?"

"Shh! Someone's coming!" I heard him scramble away from the vent.

SILENCE.

Then a single, solitary, GUN SHOT.

Chapter
+2 Hours

The gunshot stunned me. Was it for Isaac? Was it outside in the hallway? Was it even on his floor or mine? The location the shot came from wasn't clear to me and the thought that it may have hit Isaac or Eli…or hell, anyone else threw me into a pit of sorrow. I sat holding my knees, rocking for I'm not sure how long—staring at the blinking blue light on my phone before it even registered that I had received a new email.

Grabbing my phone I straightened up as I swiped the screen. 9:18. I tapped the email icon indicating I had three new emails and tapped on the first.

SUBJECT: RANSOM NOTE
TO:
RheaVelvetKenzee@pacificlakescommunityc
ollege.us.net
FROM:
EliValenSnohe@pacificlakescommunitycolle
ge.us.net
SO, YOU PLAN TO KIDNAP ME
EHH? SOUNDS LIKE A PLAN I COULD
GET BEHIND 110%. HAHA (…MMM, I
LIKE THE IDEA OF GETTING BEHIND
SOMETHING…EHH HEMM…SOMEONE
ELSE 110% TOO).
OKAY, OKAY…PULLING MY
MIND OUT OF THE GUTTER,
ALTHOUGH IT'S HARD SINCE THAT'S
WHERE IT SEEMS TO GO ALMOST
EVERYTIME I THINK OF YOU.

…DON'T SAY ANTHING ABOUT HOW WEIRD THAT IS. I AM A GUY AFTER ALL.

SO, IF YOU'RE PLANNING TO KIDNAP ME AND TORTURE ME WITH YOUR KISSES—I THOUGHT MAYBE YOU SHOULD COME UP WITH A BELIEVABLE RANSOM NOTE. RIGHT? DON'T YOU THINK?

SO…HERE GOES.

After all of the emotional and mental torture that I have endured while held hostage at PLCC I am no longer able to define behavior that is considered acceptable from behavior that isn't. With that being said, a fellow student emailed me while I was held captive and when we got out I couldn't imagine a future without him. So, I've kidnapped him.

Every hour on the hour I plan to torture him in the most wicked ways—using tools ranging from my mouth, to ropes, and canes. Eventually there won't be one area on his body that hasn't been explored by mine.

If you want to see Eli back before he is nothing more than a sated, drained shell of himself…you must pay me the sum of $1,000,000,000 dollars that can be deposited into my Swiss bank account.

The email went on, but I couldn't risk laughing aloud. Eli was simply genius. How he was able to make me smile in the situation that I was in—well, it was a feature that I was very attracted to. Still chuckling, I clicked on the next one; the recent shot still echoing in my ears.

SUBJECT: SAY SOMETHING
TO:
RheaVelvetKenzee@pacificlakescommunityc
ollege.us.net
FROM:
EsiahJosephCurn@pacificlakescommunitycol
lege.us.net
RHE,
EMM SAID SHE HASN'T HEARD FROM YOU. SHE'S WORRIED. I'M WORRIED, AND TO BE HONEST…A LOT OF THE COMMUNITY IS WORRIED. SO, WHY WON'T YOU RESPOND? QUIT THINKING ONLY OF YOURSELF. ARE YOU OKAY? WHAT'S THE SITUATION? ARE YOU ALIVE? QUIT THE SILENT TREATMENT AND UPDATE ME.
ESIAH

Oh my fucking God! Is he serious? I had never realized how narcissistic he was until now. I mean, did he not get that the world does not answer to his rules—especially not me anymore and especially not now when I have all this stuff going on?

SUBJECT: RE: SAY SOMETHING
TO:
EsiahJosephCurn@pacificlakescommunitycol
lege.us.net

FROM:
RheaVelvetKenzee@pacificlakescommunityc
ollege.us.net
ESIAH,
I DIDN'T ANSWER YOU BEFORE
BECAUSE I WAS UNSURE OF WHAT TO
SAY OR HOW I FELT. LUCKILY, YOUR
LAST EMAIL REMINDED ME OF WHAT
A DOUCHE' BAG YOU ARE.
TO ANSWER YOUR
QUESTIONS…
YES I'M OKAY.
THE SITUATION IS I NEVER
WANT TO TALK TO YOU AGAIN.
YES I'M ALIVE.
…NOW, GO FUCK YOURSELF.
~RHEA~

I just couldn't stop shaking my head as I
opened the last of the three emails.

SUBJECT: GIVE ME AN UPDATE
TO:
RheaVelvetKenzee@pacificlakescommunityc
ollege.us.net
FROM:
EmmoryVanessaJane@pacificlakescommunit
ycollege.us.net
RHEA,
SO, MOM'S BEEN IN CONTACT
WITH THE POLICE, THE GOVENOR
AND ME—FILLING ME IN ON WHAT'S
GOING ON. THE GUNMEN ARE ASKING

FOR A CRAP-LOAD OF MONEY SINCE
THEIR PLAN TO STEAL THE
COLLEGE'S DIDN'T PAN OUT.
          THAT'S NOT GOING TO HAPPEN.
          THE ARMY NATIONAL GUARD
AND SWAT TEAMS ARE MOBILIZING
FOR A RAID IN A COUPLE OF HOURS—
SOONER IF THERE'S AN IMMEDIATE
THREAT TO YOU GUYS.
          WHAT'S GOING ON IN THERE?
          *EMM

My fingers flew across the touch screen as I typed out a hurried response.

          SUBJECT: RE: GIVE ME AN
UPDATE
          TO:
EmmoryVanessaJane@pacificlakescommunit
ycollege.us.net
          FROM:
RheaVelvetKenzee@pacificlakescommunityc
ollege.us.net
          EMM,
          I'VE HAD TO MOVE. ISAAC
MATTHEWS WARNED ME THAT THEY
WERE COMING FOR ME—SO I HAD
TIME TO GET OUT AND HIDE
SOMEWHERE ELSE. IT WAS A CLOSE
CALL.
          THERE WAS ANOTHER
GUNSHOT ABOUT FIVE MINUTES AGO.
THEN SILENCE.

AND, WHY DID YOU TELL ESIAH ANYTHING ABOUT ME? ABOUT THIS? I THOUGHT FROM HIS FIRST EMAIL THAT MAYBE HE CHANGED—BUT HE'S STILL THE SAME CONTROLLING, MIND-FUCK OF A GUY HE WAS THE LAST TWO YEARS WE DATED.
THANKS BY THE WAY…SO, QUIT TALKING TO HIM ABOUT ME! GET ME OUT OF HERE!!!!!!
~RHEA~

Now that the crappy emails were taken care of and out of the way, I could focus on responding to Eli—if you could call it focusing. That single gunshot reverberated in my head, bouncing off the sides of my skull. Echoing. ECHOING.

Why hadn't I heard from Isaac yet?

Panic was palpable in the duct. If I had a knife I'd be able to cut through it.

SUBJECT: YOU'RE A FUNNY GUY
TO: EliValenSnohe@pacificlakescommunitycollege.us.net
FROM: RheaVelvetKenzee@pacificlakescommunitycollege.us.net
ELI,
HAHA.
YOU TOTALLY HAD ME LAUGHING TO MYSELF. I HAD NO

IDEA YOU WERE SUCH A COMEDIAN? I
READ YOUR LAST EMAIL RIGHT
AFTER THE LAST GUNSHOT.
       ARE YOU OKAY?
       I'M WORRIED THAT YOU OR MY
PROFESSOR OR ANY OTHER HOSTAGE
HAS BEEN SHOT.
       WHERE ARE YOU?
       I WISH I WASN'T ALONE IN
HERE…

I tapped my fingers on the wall of the duct…should I
tell him *everything* that I am thinking? I stretched out my
legs and rotated my ankles, cracked my knuckles and rolled
my head from side to side. The cramps were getting nearly
unbearable.

       SO, THERE'S SO MUCH MORE
THAT I WANT TO SAY TO YOU…
       FIRSTLY, MY EX HAS
CONTACTED ME AND ALTHOUGH HE
ISN'T IN THE PICTURE, I SHOULD
WARN YOU HE'S A NARCISSISTIC PIG
AND WILL PROBABLY MAKE OUR
LIVES HELL.
       SECONDLY, SOMEONE THAT I
HAVE LIKED FOR OVER A YEAR
FINALLY TOLD ME THAT HE LIKED ME
TOO…ONLY IT CAME AFTER YOU AND
I FELL INTO A COMFORTABLE, SEXY
AND EXCITING GROOVE; HOWEVER, I
JUST CAN'T COMPLETELY DISCOUNT
THAT THERE *ARE* FEELINGS THERE.

LASTLY, YOU MAKE ME FEEL
BETTER. WHEN I AM SCARED, LONELY,
OR NEED COMFORTING…YOU ARE
THE FIRST PERSON THAT I WISH WAS
IN HERE WITH ME. WHAT I WOULDN'T
GIVE FOR YOU TO BE ABLE TO HOLD
ME RIGHT NOW, FOR ME TO RUN MY
FINGERS THROUGH YOUR DARK
WAVY HAIR, TO KISS YOUR FULL LIPS.
ELI—PLEASE LET ME KNOW
YOU ARE OKAY. ALSO, PLEASE IF YOU
AREN'T *REALLY* THAT IN TO ME AND
THIS IS JUST A CRISIS-TYPE-FLING-
THING…LET ME KNOW?
~RHEA~

No sooner had I hit send, than a new email came
through.

SUBJECT: **KEEP QUIET!**
TO:
RheaVelvetKenzee@pacificlakescommunityc
ollege.us.net
FROM:
IsaacJoesephMatthews@pacificlakescommun
itycollege.us.net
THE GUNMEN ARE ON A
WARPATH. THEY ARE HUNTING FOR
YOU, ME, AND ANYONE THEY CAN
FIND. THEY KEEP COMING UP HERE IN
THE STORAGE AREA BELOW THE
ATTIC. I WONDER IF THEY KNOW I'M
HERE.

PLEASE, PLEASE DON'T SAY A
WORD UNTIL I CALL FOR YOU. DON'T
ANSWER TO ANYTHING EXCEPT
KENZEE…I'LL CALL OUT TO YOU BY
THAT NAME.
        ISAAC.
P.S. WORRYING ABOUT YOU IS
KILLING ME. NOT BEING ABLE TO
KNOW WHAT YOU WERE GOING TO
SHARE IS KILLING ME. DO I EVEN
HAVE A SHOT? I TRULY BELIEVE
WE'D BE SO HAPPY AND I KICK
MYSELF FOR NOT LETTING YOU
KNOW MY FEELINGS SOONER…EVEN
AT THE RISK OF LOSING MY JOB AND
FELLOWSHIP.

SILLY I KNOW, BUT IS LIFE WORTH
LIVING IF YOUR'RE NOT TRULY
LIVING? LOSING IT ALL WOULD'VE
BEEN WORTH IT IF IT MEANT THAT I'D
ALREADY HAVE YOU.

A sudden onslaught of emotions caught me off guard. Why was I so worried about who I liked and if they liked me? What I needed to be worried about was how to stay alive.

I threw my head up—looking straight into the air duct above my head. I placed my hands over my chest, trying to keep my heart from beating out of it.

TWO MORE GUN SHOTS.

Oh my God! Isaac!

I listened and after the shots that startled me went off…there was absolute silence. Trying to keep my emotions in check and my adrenaline response under control, I tapped my phone again. I had never been so glad that I had it with me, I couldn't even imagine what it would've been like being alone in these air ducts without it.

> SUBJECT: SHOTS
> TO:
> IsaacJoesephMatthews@pacificlakescommunitycollege.us.net
> FROM:
> RheaVelvetKenzee@pacificlakescommunitycollege.us.net
> I HEARD THE SHOTS GO OFF
> AND IT SOUNDED LIKE IT CAME FROM
> WHERE YOU ARE. ARE YOU OKAY?
> I'M WORRIED.
> ~RHEA~

I swiped the compose email icon and began typing.

> SUBJECT: 911
> TO:
> EliValenSnohe@pacificlakescommunitycollege.us.net
> FROM:
> RheaVelvetKenzee@pacificlakescommunitycollege.us.net
> ELI,
> I NEED YOUR HELP. EMAIL ME.
> ~RHEA~

I hit send, glanced at the screen and it read 10:10. I was just too tired, thirsty and hungry to go on. I hadn't realized how cold I was—I figured they must have the heat turned down overnight, causing my fingertips to become icicles. I quietly slid myself away from the open duct above me and laid down in a tight fetal position. My purse folded over as a pillow was sheer heaven.

Chapter
+7 Hours

I woke up shivering. The silence was deafening, the blackness heavy and deep. I slid my way back towards the duct dead-end so I had enough room to sit up. I struggled to pull my body into a sitting position and then pulling my legs under me, tried to rock up onto my feet.

OH THE PAIN! The pain was intense enough to send stars across my vision but I knew I had to try standing up. I had read enough online to know that sitting for too long was dangerous—something to do with blood clots. Actually, at this point I was so fatigued and hungry, so emotionally worn out…that who knew if I'd made this fact up or had actually read it somewhere. No matter. I forced myself up; first a squat, then half bent, until I made it up into a crooked, old man type stance—with my hands on my lower back. No easy feat considering the size of the duct.

The heat surged on and a gust of damp, ice-cold air hit me—followed by a much drier, hotter air. It hit me like a wave, crashing over me. Dousing me head first until it had washed over my entire body. I shivered it felt so good, and I swear it washed the goose-bumps I'd been wearing all night, off. I felt them disappear. Did I already mention how amazing it was?

My phone vibrated on the duct floor next to me and I bent like an old decrepit, worn-torn veteran. I swiped at the screen, 3.10 am. There was no email from Isaac, but a couple from Eli. Instead of my heart soaring, a heavy grief hit me.

Isaac's dead…

I couldn't shake the thought as I pulled the email up to read.

SUBJECT: IT'S TIME!
TO:
RheaVelvetKenzee@pacificlakescommunityc
ollege.us.net
FROM:
EliValenSnohe@pacificlakescommunitycolle
ge.us.net
RHEA,
I'VE DECIDED IT'S TIME TO
GROUP UP. THE LAST SHOTS WERE
TOO CLOSE. I WANT YOU WITH ME.
I NEED YOU TO MOVE SILENTLY
THROUGH THE DUCTS AND GET BACK
TO THE CLASSROOM THAT YOUR
TEACHER FRIEND PUT YOU IN. I'LL
MEET YOU THERE.
WHAT KIND OF HELP DID YOU
NEED?
ELI.

SUBJECT: **WHERE ARE YOU!!**
TO:
RheaVelvetKenzee@pacificlakescommunityc
ollege.us.net
FROM:
EliValenSnohe@pacificlakescommunitycolle
ge.us.net
RHEA,
WHERE THE HELL ARE YOU? I'M
HERE.
GET YOUR ASS HERE!
ELI.

SUBJECT: PLEASE BE THERE
TO:
EliValenSnohe@pacificlakescommunitycolle
ge.us.net
FROM:
RheaVelvetKenzee@pacificlakescommunityc
ollege.us.net
ELI,
I THINK ISAAC WAS SHOT.
I'M ON MY WAY.
~RHEA~

I glanced up into the vertical air duct that was my link to Isaac but nothing but blackness greeted me. I paused for a second longer, thinking that I had maybe heard 'Kenzee', but only silence hailed. I lowered myself back into the two foot by three foot duct, hung my purse around my neck, and began navigating the labyrinth of darkness with only my phone's home screen as my light. I crawled more carefully than I ever had before in my life, pausing every few seconds to listen. Making sure there were no sounds, no voices, nobody nearby.

Lefts followed rights. Dead-ends reached out to me and retreated as I surged forward towards an uncertain future, Emm's favorite song 'Soon We'll Be Found' cycled 'round and 'round in my head—bouncing off the walls of my skull.

Turn around I know we're lost but soon we'll be found...Tomorrow we'll be free...

And REPEAT. On and on I crept, the lack of light was oppressive, claustrophobic. My heart was racing, beating so loudly that at times I even found it hard to hear the song in my own head. My mouth was dry—it had long ago gone from glue-stick sticky to arid-desert dry. My lips felt like braille when I ran my fingers over them they were so cracked and dry. Always moving stealthily, stealing seconds that became long moments that I'd never get back…*that Isaac will never get back.*

Where is that vent? Shouldn't I be there by now?

My breathing came in short pants, laced with fear and I struggled to move on. I struggled to move past the blindness that my renegade tears were responsible for. I had felt my phone vibrate long ago, but I was too afraid to look. What if it wasn't Eli or Iaasc? There was a 'T' ahead and I prayed that it was the last one. Just a final left and I'd be there. My heartrate sped up and I didn't care now that I was banging along…

I. CAN'T. BE. IN. HERE. ANYMORE.

At the 'T', I took a left and froze.

Someone was there. I warily backed up as stealthily as possible. Maybe they hadn't seen me right? I mean, it's dark where I was and they had moonlight coming from the classroom, filtrating through the opening where the vent had been. I sat. I waited.

Chapter
+8 Hours

"Rhea?" A nearly inaudible whisper wafted to my ears. Had I heard correctly? I had begun to think I was maybe going crazy what with all the bizarre thoughts that I'd had playing in my mind. It was crazy how someone as sarcastic and sane as me could feel the crazies from being cooped up in the dark, confined, eerily silent air duct I had been in for close to… I pulled out my phone and stuffing it under my shirt, swiped the screen. 4:15 stared back at me. It had been almost exactly twenty hours since I had stepped foot on campus and impossibly longer since I had eaten anything or peed. Just thinking about it put me in a bad way.

"Rhea!"

That time I was positive I heard my name; I cautiously peered around the corner of the duct intersection and nearly came face to face with a man. I fell back on my ass, scrambling to get away from him. I rolled back onto all fours and scrambled to get away. I was certain that this was how I would die. My time was up.

Strong hands reached out for me and long, solid fingers wrapped around my right ankle closest to him.

It's all over.

I rolled onto my right side and kicked with my left foot as hard as I could, air gusting out of my lips as quickly as I sucked it in.

"Jeezus Rhea! Stop for Christssake!"

I froze. I quit struggling. How did the gunman know my name? Surely they had taken some sort of attendance off a class roster and I was the only girl missing.

"H…how do you know my name?" My voice was unrecognizable. Small, timid, weak—so everything I wasn't.

"Fuck. We've only been emailing each other since this damn thing started." At that, he let go of my ankle, and I pulled myself into a seated position. I didn't trust he was who he said he was…not yet. I hugged myself tightly, keeping away from him. Away from sure death.

"Jeezus Rhea, it's me, Eli." His voice softened and he rounded the corner and pulled my bundled body in tightly alongside him. I couldn't believe it. I wasn't alone anymore.

I'm not alone. I've made it. It's finally over.

I exhaled severely into his chest as he stroked my hair, tightly hugging me to him.

"Shh. Shh baby. It's all over. I won't leave you. You're not alone any longer."

I couldn't help myself and sobbed heavily. "Eli. Eli…my sweet Eli." I looked up at him and intense chemistry flowed between us. Unabashedly, wildly. It shook me even deeper to my core than the fear I had been existing in the past day. His lips lowered down to mine and pressed softly at first against my cracked, chaffed ones.

I let myself feel something other than the panic and terror I had felt every second of every minute of the last twenty hours. I kissed him back. Gently at first, then with a degree of passion that I'd only read about in those cheesy newsstand romance novels. My hands moved into his hair as I pulled him to me for an even deeper kiss. Eli responded, drawing my tongue into his mouth and caressing it with his own. His hands held my face and guided our kiss. It wasn't aggressively lustful, but a kiss filled with pent up desire and need. I needed him to make me feel safe. I needed this minute, these sixty seconds to forget about where I was, where I'd been and what I'd have to do to survive.

As he pulled his mouth from mine, he kissed my forehead. "Come on, we need to get moving before everyone wakes up."

I nodded. "Isaac, I think he's been shot."

"Your professor?"

I nodded again. "I haven't heard from him since those last two shots went off last night. I got so tired right after that I fell asleep for a short time, but when I woke up the only emails were from you." I stumbled over my words, "I mean, not that I wasn't glad you wrote me."

He cut me off, "It's just you had hoped to hear from him. I understand." I could hear the smile in his voice even if it was too dark to see him. "We really need to get out of here." He patted my leg and moved toward the 'T'. "Are you coming?"

I nodded and followed at his heels until just before we reached the vent opening. Eli went on ahead, pausing at the entrance to the darkened classroom before disappearing completely.

A moment later he was back. "Rhea? Baby, we need to move."

I crawled towards the vent opening and paused at the dead-end that I had found refuge in for so many hours.

"We *really* need to get moving." His voice was urgent, demanding me to move.

I nodded although he couldn't see me. I hesitated to step out. I couldn't explain it, but now I understood why caged animals didn't always choose to escape when their cage doors are left open. Just the vastness of the open space was daunting. Terrifying really; so was not knowing if the gunmen were around the corner.

Eli reached out for me and I grasped his hand as though it were a lifeline and I were drowning.

"That's it," he said softly, "you've got this." He pulled me to my feet and our bodies brushed for a second time, sending shock waves through my body, intense feelings flirting across my soul. He took my hand, and I followed at his heels to the rear door of the classroom.

He turned to me, "We've got to move fast. Where did you say Isaac was?"

"He said in the beginning he was heading to the attic, but we were talking to one another last night and he said he was in the storage room below the attic." I shrugged, "I had no idea where that is."

"Okay, I if it is near the attic then I know where it is. Stay on my heels, we haven't got much time."

I nodded and smiled timidly.

He quietly pulled the door open and checked the hallway lit by only emergency lighting. Nodding to me that is was clear, he pulled me through the door and down the hall. It was antagonizing how slowly we were moving, placing our feet carefully so that none of the gunmen in the room down the hall heard us.

At the first corner, we paused so he could check and then at every subsequent corner until we reached a doorway. We stopped and he nodded toward the door. I stared back at him like a doe in headlights.

Does he really expect me to go in there alone? He said he wouldn't leave me alone!

"Rhea," he said in a low whisper. "That's the door, Isaac should be there. I have to go do a check and see what's going on outside. Last I looked there were teams staging outside."

I just nodded and reached for the door pushing it carefully open. "Make it back safely."

He smiled and swooped down for a brief kiss. "I will. I've been moving around all night." He winked and was off.

I turned back toward the darkened room and stepped in, gently closing the heavy door behind me. It wasn't nearly as dark as the ducts had been and once my eyes adjusted to the lack of light—the moonlight lit things up pretty well. I moved into a dark corner and scanned the room for any type of movement.

"Isaac? ISAAC, are you there?" I whisper-shouted his name, hoping he'd hear me. SILENCE. I searched the room for the air vent and finally saw it across the room, partially showing behind a stack of boxes. If he had been talking to me from there, I'd surely see him. I reached the boxes and expecting to see him felt the bottom drop out of my stomach. He wasn't there. I sat down behind the boxes, I had to try to figure out where he was.

Minutes went past as I tried to piece together the turns that I had taken to reach the vertical air duct that I had talked to Isaac through.

Vertical air duct…VERTICAL AIR DUCT! He was above me and this room was on the same floor as me! I had to find stairs!

With a renewed sense of purpose, I stood up and scanned the room. It was a large room, big enough to hold a large lecture in, or a social dance. There were all kinds of boxes, posters, computers, classroom furniture littering the room, so I decided the best way to find the attic entrance was to trace the perimeter. I went ahead and moved forward, seeing as how I already knew there were no doors or stairwells from the direction I'd come.

The process was a bit tedious, because although I could see reasonably well, there was still a lot of stuff I had to navigate without bumping. After a few sufferable minutes,

I located what I was looking for, the storage door to the attic. I glanced back behind me, making sure the coast was clear and pulled it open. A blast of frigid air hit me—they obviously had the attic on a different heating zone. I made sure the door gently closed and pulled my phone out, sweeping the screen so the light from the home page could light my way. I noticed that I had emails, but none from Eli or Isaac; and quite frankly—everyone else could wait.

The space at the top of the old wooden stairs opened into an expansive room with exposed wooden beams and high ceilings. If I had thought the other room was littered with boxes and random shit, this room had twice the amount…at least.

"Isaac? Isaac! Are you up here?" I heard a faint scuffling, a sort of scraping noise and I followed it around several piles of boxes until I could see the far end of the room. There, laying on the ground was a dark shadow and beside it—an air vent.

Oh my God! Isaac!

I ran towards him, not even considering the echo my feet made on the hardwood floor. My only thought was he was alive. I knelt down beside him, "Mr. Matthews—oh my God Isaac, you've been shot."

Two chestnut colored eyes flickered open and blinked a few times before focusing on me. He didn't say anything, but just stared at me.

"Isaac? Please tell me you're okay?" I reached out for him, but when I touched him he jumped involuntarily. It was only then that he reached out for me.

"Rhea? Rhea is that you?"

I took his hand in mine and leaned over him so he didn't have to turn his head or strain to see me looking into his eyes. "I'm right here. Eli found me and now I've found you."

Tears filled his eyes and he gave my hand a weak squeeze. "I've been shot." I followed his hand with my eyes to his abdomen, and below his diaphragm was a large bloody stain on the upper right side closest to me.

"Jeezus, Isaac, you've lost a lot of…" My eyes swept the floor area he'd been laying on and I couldn't believe I hadn't noticed the pooled blood. "…blood."

"Rhea?"

"Shh, Isaac, you don't need to say anything. Help is almost here."

"Don't lie to me. I'm not going to make it…the blood, it's all over and I'm so cold."

I started to pull away from him, to get up and go find something to help keep him warm with but he caught my arm.

"Rhea. You're all that has kept me alive. Thinking of you and me after all of this. The possibility of us, how good it can be means everything to me. This is your sliding door; don't let our future pass you by." I placed my index finger on his lips to silence him, but he kissed it. His grip on my arm got surprisingly stronger and he was actually trying to pull me into him. "Rhea, just one. Just one kiss to tide me over."

I looked into his teary eyes and my heart ached for him. We had bonded through the duct, and I hated to see my own fear reflected back at me in his eyes. I leaned into him, scarily aware that his bullet wound was about where I was, and I kissed him. My lips grazed his in a demure kiss before I raised my head.

He chuckled and coughed as he did so, grasping his abdomen. "Aw, come on. Surely you can't let that be the last kiss I ever receive. That was pitiful."

I smiled widely and leaned in, teasing him with my hot breath as I looked into his eyes. "Isaac, you kept me alive in the duct, and I'm going to keep you alive out here." My lips met his in earnest, and as his mouth parted, my tongue slid into its warm depths. Our tongues danced, pulling and drawing from the other. For a gunshot victim, he sure could kiss. When I finally raised my head, I was nearly as breathless as he was.

"Dear God…" I said breathlessly.

"I've been praying to him all night myself." The cutest playful smile flickered across his lips before his body started shaking uncontrollably. I ran my hand across his forehead and hopped up. Immediately my eyes found a heavy moving blanket that had been laid over some print billboards for protection. I whipped it off and rushed back to Isaac, covering him. Praying it would stop the shivering.

My Grand-Mimi had been young for her age and I had gone to her when she was only in her early forties. She'd met and been devoutly loyal to Jessie, an EMT. They had never married, but that was only because she had been married to the role of raising me. They stayed together until I was a senior and he passed from a tragic gunshot wound he had received on the job. But one of the things she had encouraged was our relationship and I thought of him as a father—even if he wasn't. He had taught me many things back in the day that I had filed in the useless file, but seeing Isaac laying there in a pool of blood—well I accessed the *ABCDE* file he had taught me.

Airway—I quickly assessed whether Isaac's airway was unstable or at risk, but saw no need for intervention.

Breathing—I assessed his breathing sounds, rate and depth. I listened to the sounds of his breathing and noted they were shallow.

Circulation—well, that was the obvious one. He'd lost a lot of blood and would most definitely need several units once they got him to the hospital. I checked the rate, regularity, strength and quality of his pulse and made a note that it was weak and fluttery. He was in a dire situation if he didn't receive help soon.

Disability/Neurological—He was alert to verbal stimuli and responsive to pain.

Expose—I did a quick evaluation of his body, pulling the blanket and his clothing aside. I found that he'd held a now saturated sock to his bullet wound in his upper abdomen for some time—probably until he'd passed out or gone into shock last night. I didn't find another bullet wound and was relieved that of the two shots fired, only one had hit him.

I completed the *ABCDE* assessment and looked back at Isaac. His eyes had already gotten glossy again since I had started my evaluation, and I wondered just how much blood he'd lost. He seemed to be slipping away.

I leaned back over him and whispered, "Don't you dare die on me, Isaac! Not after everything we've been through. Don't you dare die."

His eyes rolled back into his head and his breathing shallowed. I leaned in to make sure he was still breathing.

"…love yo…" the last two sounds he breathed out before he went silent.

Oh sweet Jeezus! No. No…you couldn't be…

I sat back on my heels, watching him, looking for evidence he was still breathing—there, a breath; as shallow as it was—he'd only passed out.

For now. I sighed a breath of relief.

I moved to the other side of him and laid down, pulling the blanket over our heads, and snuggling in closely. He'd lost so much blood I wanted to make sure he didn't slip into hypothermia, and if I could keep his core temperature up through our body contact and a warmer environment…well—hell, he'd have less of a chance of hemorrhaging.

Thank you Grand-Mimi for Jesse!

As I lay there snuggling in to him, enveloped in his scent, there. Right there was where I needed to be. Exactly where I wanted to be.

Chapter
+10 Hours

I must have dosed off. Being under such emotional duress and being snuggled in tightly to a fine specimen of a man will do that to you. I smiled—*really?* Never mind, being snuggled up against a sexy man has never put me to sleep before. I was curious where Eli was. *What time is it? How long have I been out?* I couldn't bring myself to move from the warm cocoon I'd fashioned. Light was visible through the blanket, so I knew it had to be after six in the morning—the sun was up.

"You're awake." The gravelly voice beside me sounded so pained, so finite that I raised on my elbow to look into his eyes.

Those eyes that I had gotten lost in many times over the past two years, were focused pointedly, directly at me.

"It feels better than I'd imagined having you like this…by my side I mean."

"Shh, just rest." I was beyond relieved that he was hanging in there. I was well aware that the liver and gallbladder were in the vicinity of his wound, and gauging the amount of blood he'd lost, they'd probably been compromised. If my estimation on the time was right, he'd been shot over eight hours ago. It was superhuman that he was still alive let alone talking to me.

"I'll have plenty of time for rest—I want, I want you to know somethings." he said unevenly, pausing to suck in a shallow breath. "I've had a lot of time to think." His breathing was shallow, and his words were coming out in gusty exhales. I could tell he was having a hard time talking, but was expending the effort because he felt it was important.

I smiled genuinely at him. Earlier I had told him that my heart had been filled, but that I wasn't against the possibility of us; so, didn't I at least owe him these precious moments?

"You're so beautiful."

I blushed, thankful he couldn't see it in the dim light under the blanket we were still cocooned under.

"You know, I noticed you when you toured campus as a high school senior nearly three and a half years ago. I was finishing up my senior year and looking at options for my future in Advertising and Journalism. I choose the Ph.D route, but having you in my classes was a benny for sure." He coughed, grabbing his abdomen as waves of pain rolled across his face.

"Shh. You need to rest. We can talk about all of this later."

"Rhea. You and I both know there may not be a *later.*"

I couldn't resist, and I reached out—running my chilled fingertips over his forehead, across his eyebrows, gently down his nose to his lips. I slid my hand to cup the right side of his face, lowering my head to within inches of his face. "Can I kiss you Mr. Matthews?"

"I thought you'd never ask." His left hand that was sandwiched between our two bodies, lifted and rested on my hipbone, pulling me tighter to him. His hand was so warm, so strong and large that it was hard to distinguish dream from reality. *Am I dreaming? Was he really shot? Maybe this was all a nightmare?* These thoughts flashed through my brain like bolts of lightning. All I knew was in our cocoon, I felt safe. Happy even.

I leaned in, closing the distance between us, never taking my eyes off his as our lips met. His left hand on my hip dropped its hold as I rolled my left leg over his. His right hand limply reached up, settling on my thigh that was draped over his own, finding strength to grip me more firmly that he should've been able to…considering his condition.

Our lips danced with one another's, our tongues flirted and our teeth nipped. Holy hell he was *not* a guy shot, lying on the floor in a pool of his own blood. Was he? I broke-off our intense, passionate kiss for fear that he couldn't breathe.

"Your heart's racing—that's a bad thing considering you've already lost so much blood." I said, fear and concern palpable in my tone.

"Don't remind me. Rhea, just one more?" His left hand was pulling my ass even higher and tighter into his own hip. In spite of his injury, he was sporting an impressive erection that I could feel against my inner left thigh I'd draped over him. My apex clenched with need.

"Isaac…"

"Rhea, just because I've been the consummate instructor, doesn't mean that I didn't develop feelings for you."

"Isaac, how…I mean, look at me." I reached up to try to fix my hair.

"I am looking at you." His eyes were so clear, so intently focused on me that now it was my breath that came in shallow gasps.

"I know you think that my feelings for you all stem from this experience, Rhea. But that's simply not true. I've loved you since I first asked you about why you chose advertising two years ago and you answered that if you couldn't be a doctor and improved people's lives that way, then you wanted to influence them through smart, honest ads." His lips turned up in a wicked smile. "That's right, I broke the Cardinal Rule—never fall for a student." He coughed, and again I saw intense pain register in his eyes.

"Shh, Isaac. Rest please. You're worrying me."

"Oh stop it. I'm fine—and I need for you to know this. I want you to understand that I never approached you before yesterday with this, for two reasons. The first is I am under extreme scrutiny by faculty members, other graduate students, and my own students. My hope for a tenured position as an Assistant Professor weighs heavily on everything I do, and I NEVER wanted you to feel like you didn't earn your grades from me, or that you needed to *perform* to get the grades you so desired. We've spoken, and I knew that you'd planned on working on your Master's…so I knew there'd be time. Time for me to reveal myself to you—and don't think I haven't caught those looks you've given me—that you've always given me…and those flirtatious smiles."

Oh wow! He had noticed that I was sending him signals…

He paused long enough to shift slightly and place his hand over his wound. He must be in so much pain—I couldn't even wrap my brain around it.

"Secondly, and in spite of the signals I *thought* I was reading from you; I feared rejection. I was nervous as hell that if I went out on a limb like I am today and told you how much I really liked you that you'd laugh it off and that would be that. I mean, there's a lot of girls who just like to dangle the bait, but once you go after it, they throw you back in the pond…so-to-speak."

I nodded and rubbed my fingers across his lips. Isaac was an incredible man, and here he was telling me—*me*—how much he wanted me!

"So, what I'm trying to say, is that I know you. I have watched your interactions with others in small groups, I've heard your contributions in small classes and large lectures, and I have read numerous papers of yours. I am taken by you Rhea Kenzee—really taken—and I love everything I know about you…even down to the last tack, and *even* when you come to me for more time because of some silly mishap with your assignment or because you've procrastinated and can't turn in a half-ass project." He paused long enough to draw in a shaky breath. "Rhea, do you see those flashes of light? Do you hear the waves rushing towards us? We should get up."

I looked up from Isaacs lips that I had been transfixed on and into his eyes. They had glossed over. Panicked, I reached over to check his pulse as his hand fell away from my ass. His chest heaved heavily, sucking in shallow breaths.

"Isaac. Isaac! Stay with me baby! Stay with me! I need you here. Jeezus, stay with me…" my voice cracked, choked out by sobs. I threw back the blanket and there was Eli not five feet from me standing. He looked panicked.

"Eli? You've been here? For long?"

He shook his head, "No. Just long enough to hear him making no sense. I just got up here, the swat teams have already started to move."

Just then there was a loud bang as the door to the attic was thrown wide and heavy footsteps ascended the stairs. Eli rushed over to where I was lying and knelt down beside me. I looked into his blue eyes, now dark with fear. "You led them to us?" He caught the betrayal in my voice.

"No. No…I, I was just trying to find out details and got caught on the other side of the building. I thought I had a break so I went for it, and they must have seen the door to the storage room close. I would NEVER jeopardize you or place us as risk. Why would you even think that?" The hurt in his voice was tangible.

"You were gone for so long," I choked out an accusation. The hurt that splayed across his face stung me. "Eli…I'm so…"

"Well, well, well. What do we have here?" I knew that voice, it was the voice of the ring-leader Mercy. "Thought we wouldn't find you ehh?" He looked pin pointedly at me. Dark, cold, unfeeling eyes devoured my own timid ones. "I knew you'd come out of the walls eventually. I set the bait, and like the rat you are…you took the cheese."

Was he referring to Isaac? He had shot Isaac to lure me out?

I was reeling from my realization and I heard him talking but couldn't make heads or tails of it. Isaac might die because of me. Life was so fucking unfair!

"Bitch, on your feet!"

I looked up at him as he advanced menacingly on me. Eli was already up and extending his hand to me. Mercy walked over and rammed the butt of his AK-47 into his lower back, dropping Eli to his knees with a pained wail.

That is it! I've had it.

"Who the fuck do you think you are!" I screamed in a voice much stronger than my own.

Mercy's eyes narrowed. "I'm the guy that's gonna teach your bitch-ass mouth a lesson." He continued to leer at me as he stalked me; again I felt like prey.

I glanced in Eli's direction where he was still lying crippled on the attic floor, shaking my head, my eyes willing his not to do anything stupid. Mercy reached me and yanked me up. I fought him and protested, but he was just too large. He took me to the end of the room and threw me down on the ground below the window. The sun was streaming in— the light warmed my face.

"On your knees bitch!" I hesitated. I knew what was coming but somewhere in the back of my mind, I was hopeful that it wouldn't really happen to me. He motioned with the barrel for me to obey him. Once I was on my knees, he slammed the muzzle into my temple as he undid his fly with his other hand. His small cock fell out of his pants. I looked at it and back up at him.

"FUCKING SUCK IT BITCH. SUCK IT UNTIL IT'S HARD." I cautiously went to put my hands around it and was drawing it to my mouth when he took a fist full of my hair and crammed my face into his crotch. The stink of sweat and musk were overwhelming and bile rose into my mouth. I struggled to choke it down as he struggled to force my jaw open and cram his limp dick in my mouth. Taking a better fistful of my hair, he yanked my head back. Thank God it was small because he kept cramming and thrusting that thing into my mouth.

I let the fight go out of me, my eyes hazed and I moved robotically. It was as though I was watching a low-budget rape porno. He had my head at his control, and he was slamming my mouth into his cock with every forceful thrust he made.

"That's right bitch, just like that. Take it all, take it all."

The next few seconds felt like someone had my life on fast-forward. Out of nowhere, I saw Eli from the corner of my eye clock Mercy in the head with a piece of wood, and he crumpled on me like a wet towel. I struggled to get him off of me as the window I was directly below imploded with the force of the SWAT team as they shot through the pane.

Mercy was hauled off of me by two heavily armed officers as the others swept the room. I could hear him fighting them and voices coming up the stairs shouting and yelling for Mercy. Tears streamed from my eyes. Hot. Angry. Scared tears fell with no apologies.

Is this really almost over?

I shook my head trying to clear the mental fog that had wrapped around my brain, and Eli came into view. He knelt beside Isaac and was alternating pounding on his chest and giving him breaths. I looked up at the officers restraining Mercy and the depth of hatred that stared back at me from those dark pools chilled me to the bone. The fog began to encroach on my vision, it drew everything in and began to spin. I hear a gunshot fire twice in rapid succession…

"I'm going to come for you bitch! Bitch—do you hear me? If it's the last thing I do, I'm coming for you."

Mercy's threat was the last thing I heard before I blacked out.

Afterward

Beep. Beep. Beep. Beep.

Am I dead?

I strained to lift my eyelids and the intense fluorescents assaulted my already dimly focused and blurred eyes. I struggled to push myself up into a seated position, but shearing pain splintered through my brain and my shoulder protested.

What the fuck?

"Hey, Rhe…don't move." Blinking and confused, it was unclear who was talking to me; he was familiar but I couldn't place his voice. "I'm so glad you're okay. After you were shot, I was sure that I'd lose you."

What? I was shot? When? How? Who?

Unanswered questions rapidly fired through my brain as I tried to lift my hand to my face, but it barely moved. I willed my eyes to clear—just to be able to see who was at my side—who's been by my side.

"Rhea? Can you talk? The doctor said that it would be touch and go for a while, but I was hoping, praying actually that you've made it into the clear."

"Eli?" The feeble, raw sound that escaped from me in a squeak was *not* me.

"Yea, Baby. It's me. Thank God you're talking."

"What…" An intense, searing hot pain shot through my brain, forcing me to close my eyes. I winced from the pain.

"Shh, it'll be okay. I've been here, Emmory has been by, Eisah, and some of your other friends."

I heard the hospital room door open, and rubber footsteps made their way to my bedside.

"Eli," the deep voice began, "There's no next of kin, we've spoken with a social services representative on Ms.

Kenzee's behalf, and we need to consider other, more permanent arrangements since the likelihood of Ms. Kenzee waking up is becoming less and less of a viable…"

Eli interrupted. "Dr. Brouski, Rhea's awake."

I struggled to open my eyes against the stinging light. "Hiya, doctor." I struggled to smile, and am not sure what actually registered on my face, but the doctor sucked in a gasp of amazement.

"Holy Hell! Well, I'll be damned Ms. Kenzee! Miracles never cease to amaze me. Welcome back!"

I heard him walk hurriedly to the door, "Nurse Sumpters, Rm 803 is awake from her coma."

I heard footsteps, a barrage of people came in, took my vitals, touched me. I felt hands on my face, but they were familiar hands, and pried my eyes open to find Eli's shining, hopeful eyes only inches from my own. I opened my mouth, trying to find my voice—to be able to say 'Thank you for being here. Thank you for getting me through this. For loving me.' but my mouth and mind refused to cooperate.

"Shh, love. My precious, Rhea. You did it, you beat the odds baby. We have nothing but the future ahead of us."

"Eli…" I manage, "Isaac?"

"I love you, Rhea."

Eli's loving, compassionate, and troubled voice held promise for the future, but also shrouded secrets he wasn't yet ready to share with me. Darkness enveloped me, and I sank back into a deep, but this time restful slumber.

Look for: Volition
A Uniform & Lace Romance
Book One of Noah & Tessa's Story

Coming soon: Vexed
A Uniform & Lace Romance
A Novella in Noah & Tessa's Story

Coming soon: Veneration
A Uniform & Lace Romance
Book Two of Noah & Tessa's Story

Coming soon: Tina Maurine's story in: Kissing
Midnight
A New year's Crazy Ink Anthology

Excerpt

Volition

A Uniform & Lace Romance
Noah & Tessa's Story
~Book One~

All Rights are Reserved and Copyrighted © 2018 by Tina Maurine
(Excerpt shortened from final publication.)

Ari walked up with drinks for the three of us. He sat down on the shore with his. I took mine, leaned back on my elbows and closed my eyes, taking a long drink.

"Perfect," I purred. "Thank you, Ari. It's just what I needed… a drink to get over my hangover." I smiled at him sincerely and winked before dreamily closing my eyes. Even holding my glass, and with my elbows in the soft silica mud, my legs floated effortlessly on top of the hot mineral water. No trace of my headache lingered.

"So, baby girl, did you ever figure out who Noah Garren and Dirk Archibladt were?"

I peeked at him under hooded eyes as he jounced his eyebrows playfully up and down.

"Dirk, no, but there's something about Noah…"

"Are you effin' kidding me?" Sam shot me a look like I was slow as I moved back away from the group a bit into even shallower water. I didn't want to have to worry about getting the seawater in my drink as I half reclined with one elbow in the mud, my legs floating out in front of me. I closed my eyes, cogitating on her snide comment and judgmental look, but they did nothing to my mood—I was healing from my hangover—as I absorbed the heat, steam, mud, my elixir… everything. I wasn't going to let her ruin my good mood. It had taken me all morning to get it.

A strong hand glided up my left calf. My eyes flew open and Mr. Familiar-For-Some-Reason Noah sprawled on his elbows in the mud floating beside me. He smiled, and I noticed how straight and pretty his white teeth were; a good sign that he didn't chew or smoke. He walked himself up on his elbows until he reached shoulder to shoulder with me. I took my time *once again* admiring his tanned, rugged good looks, thick hair, strong shoulders and back, nice firm ass and killer legs. His legs extended a good ten to twelve inches or so past mine, so he was about a foot taller than me, easily over six feet. I'd have to see him standing to be sure.

He smiled a shit-eating grin at my blatant perusal, before turning over onto his back. As my gaze combed back up his body, I noticed his strong thighs, taut six-pack, and an amazing chest that had a hint of ink hiding under the silica mud that covered most of his body. His chuckle brought me back from my lollipop walk down his yummy body.

"Like what you see?" Noah gave me a notably arrogant smirk. Then it dawned on me… his voice. It was the same husky baritone that had whispered in my ear last night after the last dance. Those amazing hands had been on my hips. The real kicker though—those full, sensual lips and already nipped at my neck. My nipples grew hard at the thought. Now, it was my turn to blush.

What were the fucking chances Ari would invite him? A million to one? How could he know? He wasn't even at the club. If he had known, would he have invited him?

"I could ask you the same thing," I countered back flirtatiously, successfully playing off an arrogant indifference just for the fun of it.

"I knew you'd look good, but had no idea… I mean, damn." His honest admission caused crimson to creep across his cheeks and ears in a blush I wouldn't have expected from this hunk of a man. He was, after all, security, and many of them had been Special Ops or skilled Artillerymen who had seen action on previous tours, and *I* had made *him* blush. It brought a genuine smile of victory to my lips.

"You never did answer me," he prodded back.

"Well shit, Noah—what do you think?" With that, I arched my back, dipping my hair in the water and thrusting my chest into the air. I closed my eyes and inhaled deeply. *God, the water feels amazing.* Its heat eased the tension in my achy, hung-over muscles and felt luxurious as it gently swathed my throbbing head. *Right now, there's no place I'd rather be. I'm so glad I came. I'll have to make sure to thank Ari for such an incredible hangover cure.*

I felt Noah's confidence radiating from every pore in his body; our chemistry undeniable, mutual sexual tension so thick you could cut it. He sidled up, saucily—hip to hip with me and turned on his side, his package firm against my hip, and draped his forearm across my taut abs. His hand rested on my hip farthest from him as his fingers gripped me in a possessive gesture. "Maybe you'll give me the chance to take you out on a real date?"

I opened my eyes and saw intense, hopeful ones looking back at me.

Acknowledgements

First I want to thank God for instilling my love of writing and for giving me the gift of expression through writing. There were many times I wondered if I were on the right path, but I always came back to Him and when I did I became refocused and confident in my choices. Writing centers me and genuinely makes me happy.

To my family—my husband and kids—who never complain when my face is staring at a screen and my hands are making music on the keys. You're never angry that my spare time—and sometimes even family time—is spent writing stories and creating other worlds. Thanks for understanding and always supporting me.

To Erin…and the team at Crazy Ink. Thanks so much for letting me express myself and for loving my form of crazy. Like you say, 'it takes all kinds!' Thanks for believing in this book and for publishing it.

To Simone…you always frost my work, put the icing on the cake. We work so well together that it's always seamless. Thanks again for making time for me in your already too-full schedule, and for an amazing blurb lady!

To Bec…it's a marvel I found you. Thanks for being there amidst your busy life and hectic schedule. The gift of your time is as invaluable to me as is your feedback. Thanks for working this through with me and making my work shine.

To Kristi…for ALWAYS making time for me. You're my biggest reader and best critic. Thanks for reading everything I throw your way. Love ya!

Lastly, to Jude, Mary, Kristi, Simone, and all the other women who support me by pimping my books, THANK YOU! THANKS TO ALL the others who have read my books and reviewed them. Without your help, I'd never sell a book. So again, thank you!

About the Author

Tina Maurine is the gal on the sidelines at the party. The gal who smiles at everyone, but rarely initiates conversation; never the center of attention, but always taking notes on those who are. She loves watching people, their authentic responses to everyday occurrences and in turn has turned years of notes into fodder for her stories, an encyclopedia of emotions and character traits that come alive on the page. She never feels more alive than when she is creating; be it stories, music, graphic art, or painting rocks and canvases with her daughter.

She is a wife, mom, best friend, secretary, teacher, cheerleader, house-straightener, chef, chauffeur, video game playing, Barbie doll dressing domestic multi-tasker. She likes her French baguettes crispy, her beer dark, and her chocolate even darker. Her music tastes are eclectic, but if there's a beat, you can bet her body is moving to it… even in the car… and the louder the better.

Tina Maurine lives in Oregon with her amazing husband of twelve years, and their two beautiful children. Prior to marriage and children, she served eight years in the United States Navy and saw the world. She and her husband share their love for travel with their kids, and take as many family trips as their busy schedules allow. When they aren't hitting the road or the skies, and when she isn't teaching, Tina is content to sit at the table in their backyard with her keyboard or a good, sexy book, and watch the kiddos play.

Follow her on Twitter and Instagram @ TinaMaurineAuth
Email: tinamaurine@hotmail.com
http://facebook.com/tina.maurine.1
http://tinamaurine.com